Henry Winkler and Lin Oliver

HANK ZIPZER

The World's Greatest Underachiever

A Tale of Two Tails

Cover illustration by Jesse Joshua Watson

GROSSET & DUNLAP
Published by the Penguin Group
Penguin Group (USA) Inc., 375 Hudson Street, New York, New York 10014, USA
Penguin Group (Canada), 90 Eglinton Avenue East, Suite 700, Toronto,
Ontario M4P 2Y3, Canada (a division of Pearson Penguin Canada Inc.)
Penguin Books Ltd., 80 Strand, London WC2R 0RL, England
Penguin Group Ireland, 25 St. Stephen's Green, Dublin 2, Ireland
(a division of Penguin Books Ltd.)
Penguin Group (Australia), 250 Camberwell Road, Camberwell, Victoria 3124, Australia
(a division of Pearson Australia Group Pty. Ltd.)
Penguin Books India Pvt. Ltd., 11 Community Centre,
Panchsheel Park, New Delhi—110 017, India
Penguin Group (NZ), 67 Apollo Drive, Rosedale, North Shore 0632, New Zealand
(a division of Pearson New Zealand Ltd.)
Penguin Books (South Africa) (Pty.) Ltd., 24 Sturdee Avenue,
Rosebank, Johannesburg 2196, South Africa

Penguin Books Ltd., Registered Offices:
80 Strand, London WC2R 0RL, England

Doodles by Theo Baker and Sarah Stern

Library of Congress Cataloging-in-Publication Data

Winkler, Henry, 1945-
A tale of two tails / by Henry Winkler and Lin Oliver.
p. cm. -- (Hank Zipzer, the world's greatest underachiever ; 15)
Summary: Fifth-grader Hank enters his dachshund Cheerio in a contest to choose a new
mascot for his school.
ISBN 978-0-448-44378-2 (pbk.) -- ISBN 978-0-448-44379-9 (hardcover) [1. Dogs--
Fiction. 2. Schools--Fiction. 3. Behavior--Fiction. 4. Contests--Fiction.] I. Oliver, Lin. II.
Title.
PZ7.W72934Tal 2008
[Fic]--dc22

2008033806

ISBN 978-0-448-44378-2 (pbk)   10 9 8 7 6 5 4 3 2 1
ISBN 978-0-448-44379-9 (hc)   10 9 8 7 6 5 4 3 2

To the parents and teachers who really UNDERSTAND the child who learns differently. You are POWERFUL. And to Stacey always.—H.W.

For Annie and Dexter, may your tails forever wag.—L.O.

CHAPTER 1

"Good morning, boys and girls," my teacher, Ms. Adolf, said as we settled into our seats for the school assembly. "I'd like to introduce you to my dear partner and beloved companion, Randolf Bartholomew Irving Adolf."

I grabbed my best friend, Frankie Townsend, by the arm.

"I can't believe what I just heard," I whispered to him.

"What did you hear that I didn't hear?" he asked.

"Ms. Adolf just told us her whole story. As in the divorce. The painful breakup followed by the months of loneliness, and at last, remarriage to her beloved longtime companion, Randolf."

"You've gone cuckoo, Hank," my other best

friend, Ashley Wong, whispered. "You've been watching too many soap operas."

"I think you need an ear cleaning," Frankie added.

"I think I understand why the first Mr. Adolf dumped her," I went on, ignoring them. "She probably graded him on how he ate dinner."

Luckily, before I could think more about the disgusting details of Ms. Adolf's social life, she leaned into the microphone and continued.

"Please give a PS 87 welcome to my award-winning thoroughbred boxer, Randolf, better known in my household as Pookie Doodle," she said.

"What a relief!" I whispered to Frankie. "Her beloved is a *dog*."

Between you and me, I have a really good imagination, but even I was having a hard time picturing Ms. Adolf in love. Just the thought of her in her grey shoes and grey dress, holding hands and walking through Central Park on a grey day, pausing for a little kiss by the side of the . . .

Stop it, Hank. Stop it right now! You're going to make yourself throw up!!!!

Randolf—oh excuse me . . . I mean Pookie Doodle—was led onto the multipurpose room stage by our principal, Leland Love. Oh, excuse me again. It was actually Randolf who was leading Principal Love. And let me just say, "leading" would be a gentle word for what that dog was doing. Randolf, who was the size of a small tugboat, was dragging Principal Love toward the edge of the stage at a very rapid pace.

Ms. Adolf bolted out from behind the podium, grabbing Randolf's leash and the back of Principal Love's jacket at the same time. It's a good thing she acted fast, because old Principal Love was about one second away from doing a major face-plant on the hardwood floor below. He gave Randolf a fake smile, the kind people in the park give to dogs that growl at them.

"His canine legs are quite well developed for a dog of the canine species," he observed.

Principal Love was trying to appear cheerful, but I could tell he was afraid of Randolf because the mole on his cheek, which is shaped like the Statue of Liberty without the torch, turned a fearful shade of burgundy. If you looked really close, you could see that mole shaking, and I'm not kidding.

"Come to mama," Ms. Adolf said to Pookie Doodle. "You're such a handsome boy. Such a good boy. Such a mama's boy."

Pookie Doodle seemed to like this kind of gooey talk, because drool started to pour from his face like the Nile River.

It was really funny to see grouchy old Ms. Adolf talking in that sweetie-baby-cutie-pie tone of voice. In the twenty-three years Ms. Adolf has been teaching at PS 87, not one student has ever heard her utter the words "good boy." Or good anything, for that matter.

Ms. Adolf, holding Randolf's leash with a grip of steel, took him back to the podium and tapped on the microphone.

"Pupils, I would like your undivided attention," she said. "Now."

When Ms. Adolf says "now," it means five minutes ago. So we all tried our best to stop laughing.

"I suppose you're wondering why Pookie Doodle has graced us with his attendance at our assembly today," Ms. Adolf said.

"I know," Luke Whitman called out, shooting his arm into the air. "Because we're having an ugly dog contest."

Well, that did it. Everyone cracked up, even the teachers. Mr. Sicilian, the fourth-grade teacher, was laughing. Mr. Rock, our music teacher, was laughing. Principal Love's mole was even laughing. (You can tell because it looked like it was doing the hula.) Only one person in the whole auditorium wasn't laughing.

You guessed it.

The grey queen herself, ladies and gentlemen—may I present the non-laughing Ms. Fanny Adolf.

"Pookie Doodle and I do not find that remark funny, Luke," she said. "It is especially offensive in light of the fact that the Pookers here has donated his valuable time, when he should be practicing his agility training at obedience school. He wanted to come to PS 87 to help make an important announcement."

"That dog talks?" asked Nick McKelty, the bully idiot of all time. "My dog talks, too . . .

in three languages. English, Spanish, and he can bark in Italian."

Yup, there it was. The McKelty Factor at work. With that guy, it's always truth times a hundred. I've seen that ratty little Chihuahua of his, and I can tell you this. He can barely bark, let alone bark in Italian.

"Pookie Doodle and I are here to announce that one week from today, PS 87 will be holding its annual Pet Day," Ms. Adolf went on. "You are all welcome to enter your pet in the competition to become the school mascot for the year."

"But I don't have a pet," Ava Turrisi, a first-grader with really tight pigtails, said.

"Then clearly, you won't be entering the competition," Ms. Adolf answered. I felt really bad for little Ava.

"My cat coughed up a fur ball in the shape of Florida," called out Rob Reinis, a tall second-grader with a big head.

"And your point, Mr. Reinis, is exactly what?" Ms. Adolf said, staring him down with her beady grey eyes.

"I just wanted you to know," the poor kid answered.

"Are there any relevant questions?" Ms. Adolf said, ignoring him.

"I have one," Katie Sperling said, raising her beautiful hand, which is attached to her beautiful self. "Does it have to be a real pet, or can I enter my stuffed autograph dog? It's baby blue with a rhinestone collar."

Ashley leaned over and whispered in my ear.

"I helped her make that collar," Ashley said. "I let her have some of my best tricolor rhinestones."

"The animals in the competition will be judged on beauty, obedience, and intelligence," Ms. Adolf said. "And I'm afraid your stuffed toy does not possess the latter."

"But he has Justin Timberlake's autograph across his tail," Katie Sperling said.

"Well, I'm sure your little pre-teenage crushes look wonderful on your bedspread, but that's where they should remain," Ms. Adolf said.

"I bet you a million dollars Ms. Adolf has never even heard of Justin Timberlake," I whispered to Frankie.

I swear, Ms. Adolf has two sets of eyes. One set watches everyone else in the school, and one set just watches me. She never misses me doing anything wrong, and me whispering during a school assembly was no exception.

"Mr. Zipzer, it looks like you enjoy talking out of turn," she said . . . into the microphone, no less! "Pupils, shall we all pause while Mr. Zipzer has a private conversation?"

That's my life, friends. In a nutshell. Everybody in the school is laughing and yelling things out, and I whisper one itty-bitty sentence to Frankie, and she's on me like mustard on a hot dog. The yellow kind, not the brown.

"I was just telling my friend Frankie that I plan to enter my dog, Cheerio," I said, hoping that if she knew I was talking about the mascot competition she wouldn't continue to embarrass me.

"I think you'll change your mind when you hear that there is one additional requirement," Ms. Adolf said.

"Nothing will discourage me and Cheerio, Ms. Adolf, from marching to victory."

"Good, because you will be required to

submit a two-page essay on the history and characteristics of your particular pet."

Whoops. I didn't see that coming.

That made no sense. I mean, why would a pet contest involve an essay? Pets don't write. Or read. And besides, just the word "essay" gives me a rash behind my knees.

But before I could present my argument to her, something unexpected happened. At least, it was unexpected to me.

It sounded like the blast of a trumpet.

"What was that?" I whispered to Frankie. "Did someone bring an instrument into the auditorium?"

Then it happened again. This time it sounded like the entire brass section of an orchestra went crazy.

I looked around to see where the noise was coming from, and then it hit me . . . right in the nose. A smell that made my eyes tear up and the hair inside my nose do jumping jacks. Honestly, I would really like to tell you what it smelled like, but there is nothing on this earth I can think to compare it to. Maybe three-month-old broccoli. No, that smells like fresh perfume compared to this. Garbage that's been wrapped in Nick McKelty's gym socks that haven't been washed for a year and a half. No, that smell is too good for this.

"Hey, Ms. Adolf, your dog just farted," Luke Whitman yelled.

Everybody cracked up.

"There is nothing funny about gastrointestinal distress in animals," Ms. Adolf declared. "The expelling of gas is a natural process. It is the body's way of releasing toxins."

Thank goodness for Principal Love, because he released us into the hall, where there was actual breathable air. We all cleared the room as fast as we could, leaving Ms. Adolf, Pookie Doodle, and a cloud of doggy gas to finish the assembly by themselves.

CHAPTER 2

After our noses recovered from the assembly, Frankie, Ashley, and I went to the cafeteria for lunch. The three of us sat down at our usual table, joining Robert Upchurch, who was already there holding places for us, and started eating the pretty delicious cafeteria mac and cheese. Immediately, we launched into one of my favorite topics these days . . . names for my new baby brother or sister. Did I mention that my mom is pregnant? Well, she is. You can tell because her stomach is starting to look like she swallowed a basketball.

Even though the baby is still several months away, I'd been thinking a lot about names for it. My mom is just weird enough to name the baby something goofy like Rainbow or Sunflower. And my dad could pull something weird out of one of his crossword puzzles, like Claudius, an eight-letter name of a Roman emperor. I can hear it now . . . *Hey, Claudius, your diaper needs changing.*

I couldn't have that.

"How about Woodrow for a boy," Ashley suggested.

"Too stiff," I said.

"Flopsy for a girl," Frankie said.

"Too unstiff," I protested.

"My butt hurts," said Robert Upchurch.

We all just turned and stared at him.

"Robert," I said. "Your butt is not the topic."

"I'm just saying," Robert said, sliding back and forth on the cafeteria bench next to me, trying to find a comfortable position. "You wouldn't want me not to say."

"Oh yes, we would," we all said together.

Robert's butt problem came as no surprise to any of us since Robert is the boniest boy in the fourth grade. He just might be the boniest kid in America.

"Dude, your butt would hurt if you were

sitting on sixty-five pillows," Frankie said. "You got no personal padding."

"For your information," Robert said, adjusting his clip-on tie around his pencil-thin neck, "my body mass index is perfectly proportionate with my height and weight and foot size."

"All the same, Robert, it wouldn't hurt you to eat my leftover macaroni and cheese," Ashley said, shoving her tray at him.

"No, Robert!" I said, pulling the tray back to our side of the table. "Don't you dare touch that. You know what cheese does to your nose."

Not to gross you out or anything, but in addition to Robert's butt problem, he also has a mucous problem. Cheese makes his honker drip for weeks. Robert goes through six boxes of Kleenex a day. If there were an Academy Award for nose-blowing, Robert would win three. One for blowing. One for snorting. And one for dripping.

"Uh-oh," Frankie whispered. "Adolf alert."

Coming over to our table was Ms. Adolf herself. She was even carrying a grey clipboard to match her all-grey outfit. I guess she must have recovered from Pookie Doodle's stomach

13

eruption, because she wasn't wearing a gas mask.

"I'm here to register anyone who would like to enter the Pet Mascot Competition," she said to us. "You must provide name of pet, age of pet, species of pet, and history of breed-slash-species in essay form. Spelling counts."

There were those words again. "Essay" and "spelling." Both of them make me break out in a rash. I started scratching my elbow in anticipation of the rash that I knew was coming on. But I couldn't let a little itching keep me from entering the contest.

"I'm so glad you came by, Ms. Adolf," I said, "because one, I'd like to sign up my dog, Cheerio, a very talented dachshund, if I do say so myself. And two, I'd like to be excused from doing the essay."

She looked at me like I had suddenly started to speak Ancient Egyptian. Her body shook so much I thought her feet were going to shake themselves out of her grey shoes without even untying them.

"Mr. Zipzer," she said, trying to gain control of herself. "How could you even think such a thing, let alone ask me that question again?"

"Actually, it wasn't that hard, Ms. Adolf. I had the thought and it just came flying out of my mouth."

Ashley was in the middle of a sip of milk, and when she heard my explanation, the milk took a sudden detour and shot out her nose. That happens to her when she drinks through a straw and laughs at the same time.

"Mr. Zipzer, the essay is an essential part of communication, used in our educational system for over two hundred years. I hardly think we're going to stop with you."

"Well, if you were going to stop with someone, I would have been your guy. Hey, you can't blame me for trying."

"Oh yes, I can. And let me warn you, Henry, I expect nothing less than perfection. From you and from your elongated dog, whom I seem to remember as rather rambunctious."

"I would agree with you, Ms. Adolf, if I only knew what that word meant."

With that remark, Ashley shot another milk missile from her nostril.

"Miss Wong," Ms. Adolf said, "this

is the problem with too much laughter. I suggest you stop laughing and use your napkin immediately."

While Ashley wiped her face, I took the clipboard from Ms. Adolf and entered my name and Cheerio's name. The third column asked what kind of pet you were entering, and at first, I started to write dachshund, but I stopped short when I realized I had no idea how to spell it. I mean, I was stumped after the *d*. So I just finished it up with a quick *og* and with that, Cheerio was an official contestant.

I handed the clipboard back to Ms. Adolf, who spun on her grey heel and took off to torture another table.

I pushed my tray to the end of the table and cleared a space in front of me. I had business to discuss, and this was no time for dessert, even if it was pineapple upside-down cake.

"Okay, guys," I said. "Here's what I'm thinking. I'm thinking we form Team Cheerio."

"But if I'm on Team Cheerio, then I can't enter my new tadpole, Boris," Ashley said. "And that wouldn't be fair to Boris."

"You can't enter him," I said. "He's only got

one frog leg, and who knows what stage he'll be in for the competition next week. Will he be a one-legged tadpole? Or a three-legged frog? Or in the middle, a two-legged frogpole?"

"Actually, there's no such thing as a frogpole," Robert chimed in. "In science circles, we know that once the front arms pop out, the amphibian becomes known as a froglet."

"Thanks for the science lesson, Robert," I groaned. "It was really . . . what's the word I'm looking for?"

"Boring!" all three of us said in unison.

Ashley twirled her ponytail with her left hand, which she does when she's thinking hard about something. Actually, it could be her right hand. I'm not too good at telling left from right.

"Okay," she said. "I'll join Team Cheerio, but you have to explain it to my tadpole. I just hope Boris doesn't grow into a froglet resenting me."

I gave her a high five to welcome her to the team, then turned to Frankie.

"What about you? Are you in?"

"I'm in, Zip. As long as you don't make me do the boring stuff. Something is telling me that you're going to want me and Ashweena to write the essay, and save all the fun stuff for yourself."

"No way, Frankie. We'll all do everything."

"Yeah," Robert piped up. "We'll all pitch in. It'll be really fun, won't it, guys?"

The three of us looked from one to another. No one said anything, but Frankie gave me a look that said, *"This was your idea, Zip. You tell him."*

"I don't know how to break this to you, Robert," I said, trying to sound all casual. "But one of us at this table is not on the team."

"Who? Ashley?" he said. "Come on, Hank. Just because she's a girl?"

"Actually, Robert," Ashley said. "I already am on the team."

Robert looked from Ashley to Frankie.

"Hey, man," he said, slapping Frankie on the back with his bony little hand. "I'm sorry you didn't make the team."

"Actually, Robert, I'm on the team, too," Frankie said.

Robert looked at me.

"Well, you've got to be on the team, because

it's your dog," he said to me. Then he glanced around the table to see if anyone else was there. Slowly, it dawned on him. For a genius kid, Robert Upchurch can be pretty thick.

"So . . . oh . . . I guess . . . I . . . should be looking for another team, right?"

We all nodded.

The thing about a pest like Robert is that you can't hurt his feelings. He recovered in about two seconds.

"That's fine," he said, crumbling his napkin up and sticking it into his macaroni dish. "Because actually, my loyalty is to Katherine, that sleek, fascinating iguana that belongs to your sister, Emily."

"Excellent thought, dude," Frankie said. "You are definitely the reptile type."

"Funny you should say that," Robert said, "because in my dreams, I have a tail that allows me to scratch my scales."

"Wow, Robert," I said. "For the first time in my life, I am speechless. I have no idea what to say to that."

"A thought that cool leaves a lot of people not knowing what to say," Robert said.

He seemed really happy as he got up from our table and headed over to join Emily, who was just getting into the food line.

He was perfect for her. Only hard-core geeks like the two of them would take being compared to a scaly, bad-tempered lizard as a compliment.

Other kids in the cafeteria signed up, too, so just like that, before the lunch period was even half over, Ms. Adolf's clipboard went from being totally empty to having a whole bunch of full-fledged teams. And I'm happy to say that the Zipzer family represented two of them. Team Cheerio, starring the cutest dachshund in the world. And Team Katherine, starring the Queen of Scales herself.

That would be my sister Emily.

Okay, sorry, I couldn't resist. I'll do that again.

Starring the Queen of Scales herself, Katherine the iguana.

CHAPTER 3

We decided that Team Cheerio had to get to work right away. I mean, Cheerio may be the cutest dog in the world, but he's not exactly well trained. Unless you consider begging for table scraps and chewing through your new socks to be well trained. It was going to take some extra work to get him in shape if he was going to win the Mascot of the Year.

Frankie and Ashley and I were really excited to get started. We rushed out of school and didn't even stop at Mr. Kim's market for our usual red-licorice pit stop. I was hurrying so fast, I nearly ran down Mason Harris Jerome Dunn and his mom as they were coming out of Mr. Kim's. Mason is my little kindergarten pal and he was wearing, as always, his blue Donald Duck shirt and carrying a

Three Musketeers bar the size of his head.

"Hey, Hank," Mason called out. "Want a bite?"

"No time," I said to him. "We're on important school business."

"Can I come?" Mason asked, running his chocolate-covered fingers through his red curly hair.

His mom fumbled around in her bag for a Kleenex or something, so she could wipe his fingers clean. I remember when my mom used to do that. You just wanted to eat your candy bar, and there was your mom, cleaning you up before you could even finish it. Boy, it was rough being a kindergartner.

"Sorry, little dude," Frankie explained to Mason. "This is grown-up business."

"You're not a grown-up," Mason said.

"Mason, watch your manners," his mom said to him.

Ashley stooped down so she was eye to eye with Mason, and explained to him in a really nice voice. "We're not actual adults yet, but compared to you, we're closer to being grown-up."

Mason looked really disappointed.

"Hey, listen, Micro Mason," I told him. "I wish I could hang out with you and watch you take off on your sugar rush, but we're in a time crunch. By the way, are you entering a pet in the competition?"

"Uh-huh," Mason nodded. "My pet snail, Snaily."

"I didn't know you had a pet snail," I said.

"I found him in Central Park. Want to see him? He lives in my pocket."

Mason reached down into his pocket, then a funny look came over his face.

"Uh-oh," he said. "He slimed my gummy bears."

For a minute, he looked like he was going cry. I hate to see little kids cry, especially a cute guy like Mason.

"Hey, don't worry about it." I tousled his little red head. "You still have that big Three Musketeers bar left. Just don't put it in your pocket."

"Okay, Hank," Mason said. "See you later."

Suddenly, he took off down the street, with

his mom chasing him and yelling for him to be sure to stop at the curb.

We hurried down the street and arrived at our apartment building in record time. Frankie and Ashley didn't even stop on their floors. We all just rode up the elevator to the tenth floor.

I was so excited to get started on Cheerio's training that I could barely get the key into the lock on my apartment door. I tried to slip it in upside down at first, but of course, it wouldn't turn. Frankie was standing next to me tapping his foot.

"Breathe, Zip," he said. "And when you're finished breathing, you might think about turning the key right-side up."

"Just think of the key as your friend," Ashley said.

"Guys, I got the key thing under control." I slipped the key into the lock right-side up this time. "I just can't wait to get started, that's all."

I turned the key to the right. Or maybe it was to the left. You know my brain and directions—let's just say they're not best friends. Anyway, whichever way I turned it, the door opened.

"I'm home!" I shouted out just like I do every day.

No one shouted back, so I motioned for Frankie and Ashley to follow me to my bedroom, where Cheerio likes to sleep on my pillow when I'm gone. I cover it with a blanket so he doesn't shed and leave his brown fur on my pillow, which would stick to my face when I'm sleeping and make me look like I have a beard when I wake up.

On our way down the hall, before we got to my room, my dad intercepted us as he was coming out of his bedroom.

"Hi, kids. You haven't seen my new red mechanical pencil, have you?"

That's my dad, good old Stanley Zipzer. He really knows how to fire up a conversation.

"Sorry, Dad. Have you looked in the pocket protector in your blue jacket? You had a buttload of mechanical pencils in there."

"I'll take a look," he said, which was great news for me because it meant that he'd be too busy checking his pocket protector to tell me to send my friends home and remind me five

25

hundred and thirty-seven times to get started on my homework.

But I was wrong. When it comes to homework reminders, my dad does not disappoint.

"Isn't it time for you kids to go home so Hank can get started on his homework?" he asked.

"No, Dad, I need them here now because we have to get started on training Cheerio. You may not realize this, but you're looking at Team Cheerio."

"What I'm looking at is a young man who is trying very hard to avoid his school responsibilities," he said, taking his glasses off his nose and pushing them up onto the top of his head.

"No, Dad. This is about school responsibilities. Isn't it, guys?"

"Yeah, Mr. Z.," Frankie chimed in. "We're entering Cheerio in the school mascot contest."

"And we don't have much time to train him for the obedience portion of the contest," Ashley added.

"That sounds like a lot of fun, Ashley," my dad said, "but as you know, Hank is not doing well enough in school to participate in extracurricular activities. That will have to wait until he has improved his spelling and reading skills."

"But you don't understand, Dad," I said, trying not to whine. "This contest does that."

"I suppose you're prepared to tell me how prancing around with a dog will help bring your test scores up," he said.

"Yes, I am."

My dad held up his hand—fingers together, palm out—which in Stanley Zipzer speak means conversation over. But Frankie, lifelong pal that he is, ignored the hand and came to my rescue.

"Honestly, Mr. Z., this contest really will help Hank with his spelling and stuff."

"That's right," Ashley nodded, "because we have to write an essay about our pets, including the whole history of the species."

"Really?" my dad said. "That sounds very worthwhile."

Worthwhile. Yeah, this was my opening. I went for it!

"And the essay will force me to check my spelling and my punctuation and even my dangling participles," I said in an extremely confident voice. Then I flashed my dad my most confident Hank Zipzer smile, the one where I show my top and bottom teeth at the same time.

Okay, I'll be honest with you. I had no idea what a dangling participle was, but Ms. Adolf talks about them all the time, so I thought this was a good place to bring them up.

And it worked.

"Oh, dangling participles," my dad said, nodding with approval. "Very nice, Hank. In fact, I might be able to use that nifty little phrase in nine down on my Thursday crossword puzzle."

Nothing gets my dad out of my face faster than a red-hot crossword puzzle clue. Faster than you could say "forty-seven across," he was sprinting to the dining room table, where the *New York Times* crossword puzzle was waiting for him.

We moved fast, before my dad changed his mind, and quickly headed into my room. We had a dog to train, and there wasn't a minute to waste.

CHAPTER 4

I shoved my bedroom door open and whistled.

"Here, boy," I called out. "Come on, Cheerio."

There was no answer.

We went inside and I looked on my bed, expecting to see him sound asleep on my pillow. But he wasn't there. I checked all his other favorite hangout spots, like the floor of my closet, where I keep a huge stuffed flamingo I won at Coney Island by throwing ping-pong balls into little dishes floating in water. He likes to cuddle up next to the flamingo's soft neck. But he wasn't there, either.

"Here, Cheerio," I called, moving aside the straw basket I use as a dirty clothes hamper. No answer. I bent down and checked under the bed, where he sometimes sleeps with his nose tucked into my furry slipper.

"He's not here," I said. "Let's check out the rest of the apartment."

Frankie and Ashley and I went looking in all Cheerio's other favorite places. The fluffy blue rug in front of the bathtub. Under my parents' bed. On the arm of the couch in the living room.

"Cheerio, where are you, boy?"

My father called out from the dining room table. "He's not here. I sent him out for a playdate."

"A playdate," Frankie said with a laugh. "Are we talking with a girl dog?"

"I bet it's with Mrs. Seides's flirty little white poodle," Ashley said with a giggle.

"Actually, there is no girl dog involved," my dad said. "I sent him over to Mrs. Fink's apartment. I had a quarterly spreadsheet I had to finish, and Cheerio was yipping and yapping. I couldn't get my work done."

That's all we needed to hear, and we were out the door.

Mrs. Fink lives in one of the two apartments

right across the hall from us. We were at her door before you could say "quarterly spreadsheet." Not that you'd ever want to, of course.

She opened her door on the first knock. As usual, she was wearing her giant pink bathrobe, and lucky for us, she had her false teeth in. Sometimes she doesn't wear them, and her pink gums match her pink robe.

"Hi, Mrs. Fink, we're looking for Cheerio," I announced.

"Come in, kids," she said, opening the door wide. I glanced around her apartment for Cheerio, but I didn't see him. What I did see was a long, furry, moving white pillow. It seemed to have a tail wagging.

"Is that my dog?" I asked Mrs. Fink.

"Cheerio and I have spent the afternoon making cherry strudel," she said. "He got into the flour bag. Didn't you, toots?"

Cheerio wagged his tail some more, and sent a cloud of white flour flying into the air.

"You're a good little baker, aren't you, toots," she said to him.

I didn't know how to break it to Mrs. Fink, but Cheerio is definitely not the toots type. He's a guy, and who calls a guy toots? Mrs. Fink, that's who.

"Come on, toots, let's see if our strudel is done."

She scooped Cheerio up in her arms, getting her pink bathrobe all covered in the white flour that was falling off his coat like snow in a blizzard. She carried him over to the kitchen and just as she got near the oven . . .

Bing! The timer went off.

"How did you do that?" I said to her in amazement. Did the timer know that she was coming over to get the strudel out of the oven?

"I've been baking these strudels so long, I just sense when they're ready," Mrs. Fink said.

"Do you want me to hold Cheerio while you get the strudel out of the oven?" I asked her.

"No thanks, dear. He knows not to put his paw near a hot oven," she said. "He's a very smart dog."

"That's going to come in very handy," Ashley said, "because we're about to start training him for the mascot competition at school."

"Well, I'm sure he'll do very well," Mrs. Fink said.

When Mrs. Fink opened the oven door, the first thing that came out was the most delicious smell of buttery dough and sweet cherries. My nose thought for sure that it was at a party. Cheerio's did, too; I could tell by the way it wiggled back and forth at lightning speed.

"Come on, Zip," Frankie whispered to me. "We have to get started, or I'm going to run out of time before I have to start my homework."

"Okay, okay," I whispered back to him. Then I turned to Mrs. Fink.

"If you'll just hand Cheerio over to me, we'll be on our way," I said to her.

"Oh, but you can't take him before he has a taste of strudel," she pleaded.

"Maybe you could save him a piece," Ashley suggested. "Cheerio has a lot to learn and we have only a little amount of time to teach him."

I took Cheerio from Mrs. Fink's arms. I turned to go, but Cheerio squirmed out of my arms and ran back over to the kitchen counter where Mrs. Fink had placed the strudel to cool off. He just sat there panting, his tongue hanging out, staring at that dessert delight.

"Cheerio," I said in my most strict voice. "Come."

He looked at me and then his head shot right back to the strudel.

"Cheerio," I repeated, raising my voice. "We have no time for this now. Come!"

He looked at me again as if to say, "Are you kidding me?" and his head shot right back to the strudel.

"Cheerio," I said, this time sounding weirdly like my father. "You have work to do. No strudel until after you've finished your homework."

Oh my gosh. Did I say that? My mouth had turned into Stanley Zipzer's.

Cheerio still didn't move. That did it.

"Cheerio, if you want to get ahead in life, you have to take your responsibilities seriously. I am very disappointed in you right now."

Disappointed? Did I say disappointed? That's what my dad always tells me. That he is disappointed in me. And here I was, telling the very same thing to Cheerio.

Wow. It was as if my dad had come flying out of my mouth!

CHAPTER 5

LUCKY!
FUN

We decided to take Cheerio to Riverside Park for a quick first training session. He wasn't too excited to go, because he was still pretty focused on taking a chunk out of that strudel. I had to use my scarf to cover his nose and eyes to get him away from Mrs. Fink's counter and into the elevator. When we got in, the delivery guy from Yang Chow's Chinese Restaurant was just getting out to drop off dinner at Tyler King's apartment.

When Cheerio got a whiff of that kung pao chicken, he lunged for it, scarf and all. That poor delivery guy, all he saw was a green-and-black striped scarf hurtling toward him. It made him very nervous, which I can understand. I mean, most people wouldn't want a panting, sniffing scarf attacking them. So he got out of the elevator faster than you can say moo goo gai pan (which I also think I detected in that bag).

When we hit the street-level lobby, we attached Cheerio's leash to his collar, pushed open the door, and headed off down the street toward Broadway. After Broadway comes West End Avenue, and after that is Riverside Drive, where the park is. And right on the other side of the park is the Hudson River, named after some explorer who I guess was named Mr. Hudson, but I'm really not sure. If you're just dying to know, you can look it up in a history book, which I would do, but I don't have time now because as I said, we were on our way to train Cheerio and we had to start right away.

"Wait a minute, guys," Ashley said, taking my arm and pulling us to a stop. "If we're going to train Cheerio, we need treats. He's got to get rewarded every time he learns something new."

"What ever happened to just saying 'good dog' and giving him a pat on the head?" Frankie said.

"Obviously, you're not used to thinking like a dog," Ashley said.

"Ashweena's right," I chimed in. "Cheerio responds best to meat and cheese."

"Right, Zip. Like I just happen to have some meat and cheese in my jacket pocket."

"Frankie, you're talking to a Zipzer. As in the son of a mother who owns only the greatest deli on the west side of New York, which happens to have a wide selection of meats and cheeses, and also happens to be across the street from where we are standing at this very second."

"Zip, when you're right, you're right. Let's do it."

We crossed the street, walked a half a block, and there it was, the Crunchy Pickle. My mom took over the deli from my grandpa, Papa Pete, and she's worked really hard to . . . as she says . . . bring it into the twenty-first century. Mostly, that means substituting soy stuff for anything that might possibly taste good. Luckily, all the old recipes that Papa Pete created are still on sale there, too, so the business hasn't been totally ruined.

We went inside and I asked Carlos, who was working the sandwich counter, if he could give us some scraps of roast beef for Cheerio. My mom, who was in the back refilling the potato-salad bin, came out when she heard my voice.

She can hear my voice from a million miles away. She says it's Mom Radar. I say it's annoying.

"What are you kids up to?" she asked. She was wearing a big white apron with an arrow pointing to her stomach that said, "Baby below!" At least it didn't say, "Claudius below," so that was good news.

"We're going to the park to teach Cheerio some new tricks," I told her.

"You can't teach an old dog new tricks," a familiar voice boomed from one of the turquoise leather booths. "Take it from me, I know."

It was Papa Pete, my grandpa and favorite tall adult in the whole world. He was having a coffee and Danish, and reading the sports section of the *Post*. Frankie, Ashley, and I all smiled at the same time. You can't be around Papa Pete and not smile. In fact, you can't even hear his voice without smiling.

"And you're certainly not giving that dog roast beef," my mom said. "I'm trying to watch his cholesterol. Here, I'll chop up some soylami for him. It's an excellent meat substitute and much gentler on his tummy."

She took out a knife and grabbed a loaf of

some greyish, brownish, fakish meat and started to chop it into pieces.

"I'm not comfortable with you kids being in the park without adult supervision," she said.

"Then can you take us, Mom? This is really important."

"I have work to do. We're doing party platters for Mr. Kim's mother. She's arriving from Korea to celebrate her eightieth birthday."

Papa Pete got up from his booth and walked over to the three of us. He has this way of putting his arms around all our shoulders at once. It's sort of like a group hug, only not as gushy.

"You keep working on the trays, Randi," he said to my mom. "If my grandkids don't mind, I'll escort them to the park. I could use some fresh air."

"Mind?" Ashley said. "Why would we mind?"

"Yeah, you're the coolest," Frankie agreed.

Papa Pete zipped up the jacket of his favorite red tracksuit that makes him look like a big strawberry bear, put his plaid cap on his head, and we were off. I slipped the baggy full of soylami into my jacket pocket and sealed it tight, so the fumes wouldn't knock me out. No offense to my mom or anything, but her soylami smells like Nick McKelty's bad breath, which could peel paint off your bedroom wall.

Riverside Park is mostly a narrow strip of grass that runs for miles along the river. The part near my apartment has a grassy hill that we sled down when it snows, and next to that are basketball courts used by the older kids. There are some benches scattered around, and when we got to the park, Papa Pete plopped himself down on one of those and immediately struck up a conversation with Officer Quinn, our local policeman, who was walking by. I saw him pull a Danish out of his pocket, tear off half, and hand it to Officer Quinn.

As Papa Pete peeled the top off his coffee, he and Officer Quinn talked bowling and basketball. I liked the way Officer Quinn could carry on a total conversation without ever taking his eyes off everything that was going on in the park.

Frankie, Ashley, and I got right to work with Cheerio. We took him over to the strip of grass and gathered in a circle around him.

"Okay," I said, "he knows how to sit and lie down on command. What should we teach him next that will impress the competition judges?"

"Let's start with the basics," Ashley suggested. "How about rolling over?"

"Great," I said. "I saw a dog do that once on television. His trainer made a circle in the air with his finger, like this, and the dog rolled over twice."

"Go for it," Frankie said.

I held out my pointer finger, asked Cheerio to pay attention, and made a circle in the air.

Nothing.

I did it again, and this time said, "Roll over, boy."

Nothing.

So I tried a third time, twirling my finger faster and making a bigger circle. This time, Cheerio did something, but it had nothing to do with rolling over. He jumped up, licked my finger, and then scratched his rump with his back paw.

"Let's go to Plan B," Frankie suggested.

"Like, right away," Ashley agreed.

"Great idea," I said. "Anyone have a Plan B?"

We all thought a minute, then Frankie spoke up.

"How about if you do the finger twirling thing to me as if I'm Cheerio," he suggested, "and I roll over on the ground. You know, to give Cheerio an idea of what he's supposed to do."

"That could work," Ashley said.

Frankie dropped onto the grass, and I got Cheerio's attention.

"Watch this, boy. Over here. Look at Frankie. Your friend. You like him."

I twirled my finger in the air, and Frankie rolled over twice in the grass, barking as he did it. He was into it. For a minute there, I thought I was looking at a very tall, dressed version of Cheerio. Then Frankie sat up, panted, and gave a little yip.

Two teenagers who were playing basketball on the court right next to us stopped right in the middle of a shot and burst out laughing.

"Nice trick, dude!" they yelled. "What else can you do?"

Frankie is a very cool guy and is not in the habit of getting laughed at. So all he could do was give them a stupid little wave, and under his breath say to me, "You owe me, Zip. Look what I do for you. If this gets around school, I'm toast."

The problem was, it was all for nothing, anyway. Cheerio wasn't even looking. He was watching an ant try to climb up a blade of grass. I don't know why he developed that sudden fascination with bugs, but he sure couldn't take his eyes off the little critter.

"Let's use the treats," Ashley said. "We forgot all about them."

I unzipped my jacket pocket, reached in, and pulled out the baggy. I took out a piece of soylami, held in front of Cheerio's nose, and pulled it back very slowly. Then I made a circle in the air.

"Roll over, boy, and you'll get this treat. Mmmmmmmmmmmm."

Nothing. As in big, fat nothing. As in, he didn't even blink.

All of a sudden, he did do something else. However, it had nothing to do with our training. In fact, it was what you might call the opposite of what we were going for in our training.

CHAPTER 6

TEN THINGS CHEERIO DID AT THE PARK THAT HAD NOTHING TO DO WITH OUR TRAINING

1. He chased a squirrel up a tree—that is, as far as Cheerio can go up a tree, which is about an inch.
2. He did a belly flop in the fountain and scared all the goldfish that thought he was Godzilla Dog.
3. He chased a flock of pigeons until they took off. He tried to flap his legs as if they were wings, and went exactly nowhere. No surprise.
4. He attached himself to Papa Pete's tracksuit and tugged so hard he almost pulled his pants down. (I never knew Papa Pete wore racing-car boxers!)

5. He jumped into an empty baby stroller, swiped the baby's rattle, stood up on his hind legs, and did the cha-cha.

6. He fell in love with a miniature schnauzer that for some reason was wearing four little red rain boots, and it wasn't even raining.

7. He peed on six rocks, nine shrubs, five lampposts, one fire hydrant, and one little old lady who didn't notice until it was too late.

I can't go on with this list, because I got so mad at him that when he ran by me, I stepped on his leash, picked him up, and said, "That's it, we're going home."

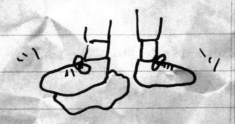

CHAPTER 7

Cheerio must have known he was being a bad boy, because when I finally caught him, he stuck his wet nose followed by the rest of his face into the crook of my elbow and whimpered.

"Let me just say this, mister," I told him in a stern voice. "Your apology is not accepted."

"You were embarrassing, Cheerio," Ashley said. "And you wasted a lot of time."

"Listen to you guys," Frankie said. "You're worse than parents. The little guy feels bad on his own. He's just a dog."

"Yeah, he's just a dog who's being irresponsible," I said.

Uh-oh. Dad voice alert. There it was again.

"Hey, kids," Papa Pete called out from the bench. "Look who's here."

It was Nick McKelty, lumbering into the

park on his tree-stump legs. You could almost hear the ground rumbling beneath his size-twelve feet. Next to this gigantoid, whose neck resembled three flagpoles tied together, was the smallest dog you've ever seen. I mean, officially it was a Chihuahua, but I'm here to tell you, that dog was just a step up from a mouse in a rat suit. If Nick didn't watch where he was going, he could mistake his dog for a pitless cherry and crush it into a fruit cocktail.

"Hey, Zipperbutt," McKelty called out to me. "You better hold on to that mutt of yours, because my dog Fang is a trained commando attack dog."

"What's he attack?" I said. "Butterflies?"

Ashley and Frankie cracked up.

"You better not laugh," McKelty said, "because Fang is trained in the ancient dog art of rip and tear."

"Fang!" Frankie laughed. "If that dog is Fang, then my name is Bernice!"

Cheerio lifted his head to glance over at Fang. I mean, not one other muscle moved except the ones he used to open his eyelids. Fang let out the wimpiest whimper you've ever heard and shot behind McKelty's leg, grabbing on to his ankle for dear life.

"Wow, McKelty, we are all just shaking in our socks," I said. "That Fang is deadly."

"You just wait until he warms up," McKelty told us. "He's back there right now sharpening his claws for the attack."

"Really?" I said. "Because it looks like there's a puddle forming at your heel."

"And it's weirdly yellow," Ashley said.

We lost it and started to laugh. Cheerio joined in, howling at the top of his lungs.

"I can't waste my time talking with you morons," McKelty announced. "I'm just going to let the contest do the talking. See if you're still laughing when Fang becomes the mascot of PS 87 for the next three hundred and sixty-five."

"Right, and my name is Bernice," Frankie repeated.

Frankie's been saying that Bernice thing since he was seven years old, but it still makes us laugh. Apparently, it works on Cheerio, too, because he started laughing even harder. It was so cute the way his lips curled up into a smile, showing his upper teeth, which reminded me that I should brush them sometime soon so he doesn't get cavities and have to go to the doggy dentist. Then they'd have to drill and that would hurt and then I'd have to go get him some special biscuits that he couldn't chew because of the novocaine and then he'd drool all over the place and . . .

"Earth to Hank," I heard Ashley saying. "Papa Pete is talking to you."

"Wow," I said. "Sorry, I didn't hear. I was lost in my brain taking Cheerio to the dentist. But we're back now."

"I was just saying," Papa Pete said, "how nice it is to see all you kids getting along so well."

What land was he living in? Oh, I know. It's the All-Kids-Get-Along-with-All-Other-Kids Land. I hear lots of grown-ups go there.

"How's your father, Nick?" Papa Pete asked.

Nick's father owns McKelty's Roll 'N' Bowl, which is one of Papa Pete's hangouts.

"He's great," Nick said. "In fact, he's meeting with the manager of the Yankees right now. They want him to play first base."

"That's strange," Papa Pete said. "Because I thought I just saw him ordering a salami sandwich at the Crunchy Pickle."

"Oh yeah," Nick said. "He was probably getting sandwiches for all the Yankees. They love salami."

That McKelty thinks he can talk his way out of anything. Papa Pete is just nice enough not to nail him on his lies.

We were all very tired from chasing Cheerio around the park, so we decided to cut the training short and make our way home.

"So the training didn't exactly take off today," Papa Pete said as we headed out of the park and over to the sidewalk. "Maybe Cheerio needs a little time to learn the commands."

"Well, while he's working on that, we still have plenty of other things to do to win the competition," Ashley pointed out.

"Like what?" Papa Pete asked. We told him about the research paper on the history of the breed that we had to do.

Papa Pete stroked his mustache.

"That's a lot of work. When are you going to get started on that?"

"Sometime soon," I said.

Frankie nudged me. "Like, now, Zip. The library's only a few blocks away. Let's swing by there and get some research books."

"Great idea," Ashley said. "We'll divide them up and all take a section."

"One problem," I said. "They don't allow dogs in the library. So I'll take Cheerio back and you guys go get the books. We can meet in the clubhouse after dinner. If that's okay, I'll see you at home."

As soon as Cheerio heard the word "home," his little ears perked straight up and his little legs took off as fast as they could, pulling me to the curb, across the street, and up the hill toward Broadway.

"See you later," I hollered. But I don't think they could hear me because we were already halfway to our building.

Let me tell you this. When a dachshund wants to get somewhere, you better get out of the way. They're short, but mighty. Come to think of it, so am I.

CHAPTER 8

Papa Pete stood on the corner and watched me go into our apartment, then walked Frankie and Ashley to the library. This worked out fine because he doesn't actually like to drop me off right in front of our apartment. He's always afraid of running into Mrs. Fink, who winks at him and invites him in to watch her DVD collection of championship bowling matches.

As I went into the building, Cheerio was still full of energy. He practically dragged me into the elevator and then spun around and around in a circle until we got to the tenth floor. The minute we reached the door of our apartment, he jumped up as high as he could and started scratching on it.

When we got inside, he bolted for the dining room table, where Emily and Robert were deeply engrossed in a project. I didn't know what it was, but I was sure it was something that they thought was smart-o-rrific, like figuring out why penguins are classified as birds even though they can't fly.

As soon as Cheerio got within four feet of Robert, the bony little kid's allergic reaction to dog hair kicked into high gear. Robert sneezed fifteen times in a row, blowing all their research papers off the table.

"Robert, I told you to number them first," Emily said. "Now we're going to have a hard time putting them back in order."

"Achoo," Robert answered. "Achoo! Achoo! Achoo!"

"Wow, Robert," I said. "I've never met anyone who defends himself in nose speak."

"Achoo," he said, just like I knew he would.

"You know that Robert has a hard time with short-haired dog dander," Emily said, which was way more information about Robert's allergies than I needed to have. "It clogs his nasal passages, which stimulates the sneeze reflex." Again, way too much information.

"I thought he was just allergic to you," I said,

hoping that would change the topic. It did, but not in a good way.

"I don't have time for your childish insults," Emily said. "Robert and I are hard at work, making sure that Katherine will become the next mascot of PS 87."

"Katherine?" I gasped. "Are you kidding? You actually think she's going to win?"

"Why not?" Emily said, giving me one of her I-am-so-superior looks. "Katherine is clearly the most talented, intelligent, and beautiful animal in the competition."

I immediately put my hands over Cheerio's ears.

"Don't listen, boy. She didn't mean it."

"Cheerio knows I love him," Emily said. "But he also knows that Katherine would make a better mascot. We all know that Cheerio could never handle the pressure of the job. He's too distractible. Just like you."

"Being distractible has its good points." I was defending myself as well as Cheerio.

"You would know," she said.

"Well, no matter what you think, I'm entering Cheerio in the mascot competition. He just had his first training session in the park, and he participated in everything that was going on around him."

I thought that was a nice way to put it. Not accurate, but nice.

"And how are you going to handle the report part of the contest?" Emily asked me. "That's not exactly your strong point."

"As a matter of fact, the research has already started. Team Cheerio is deep into dachshund history."

"Perhaps you could use this fact," Robert said, wiping his nose with a Kleenex. "Because of their elongated body and short stature, they are sometimes referred to as the wiener dog."

"Thank you, Robert, I'll keep that in mind. I really like that fact."

"Of course you do," Emily snarled, "because it's not really a scientific fact. It's more of a fun fact, suitable for someone like you who isn't really a good researcher."

"Oh really, Emily?" I couldn't let her get away with this. "You think you know everything, but what you don't know is that at this very moment, I happen to be close to four or five research books that will tell me everything I need to know."

"I don't see any books under your arm, Hank. They're not in this apartment."

"Maybe not, but they are in the building."

Luckily, this annoying conversation was ended by the phone ringing. Just as I was headed for the kitchen to get it, my dad came in from his room with the portable.

"Hank, it's Frankie," he said.

"Exactly the call I was waiting for," I said to Emily. I took the phone, put on a serious research-guy expression, and listened intently.

"Why, yes, Frankie," I nodded. "Uh-huh. That's great. And how many books do we have?"

I covered the mouthpiece and whispered to Emily. "There are so many that he couldn't carry them all. He had to share the load with Ashley."

"That's wonderful news," I said back into the phone. "Yes, of course. I'll meet you in the clubhouse at seven."

I clicked off the phone and gave Emily the old

Hank Zipzer smile. "At precisely seven o'clock, the research begins . . . Miss Know-It-All."

"I don't know about seven o'clock," my dad said. "But I do know that at precisely *now*, the homework begins. And you're not leaving this apartment until it's done."

"But, Dad, that research is homework."

"Yes, but it has nothing to do with the fractions worksheet that I happened to see waiting for you in your backpack."

Fractions! Did he say fractions? Fractions are not just hard, they're impossible!

If I had to finish that whole worksheet, I wasn't going to get to that meeting in the basement for a week and a half, unless a miracle happened and my brain suddenly kicked into gear in the fraction department.

I went into my room, sat down at my desk, picked up my pencil, and hoped for a miracle.

CHAPTER 9

Clink.

It was sound of my digital clock going from six twenty-one to six twenty-two. I had been sitting at my desk for what seemed like a year and a half, and the fractions were not getting any easier. I was still on problem two, and that's only because problem one was the sample problem and the answer was already there. Every minute seemed like an hour and every problem seemed like a puzzle with no answer.

One half minus one third equals what? Hey, I wish I knew. And besides, one half of what? One half a cantaloupe minus one third of a cantaloupe leaves a slice of cantaloupe that's delicious with cottage cheese. End of story.

Maybe they mean one half of a baseball team, minus one third of a baseball team. You can't play with one third of a baseball team, so who cares, anyway? There's nobody in the outfield to catch the ball.

Clink.

My digital clock went from six twenty-two to six twenty-three.

See what I mean? I'm never getting to this meeting in the basement.

I got up and wandered into the living room, where my dad was watching the news. I flopped down in a chair, trying to look like a guy who was just about finished with his homework.

"Hey, Dad, what's happening in the world today?"

"What are you doing here, mister?"

"I'm taking a break before my mind breaks."

"I assume you've completed your fractions worksheet," he said.

"I'm this close," I said, purposely not holding up my hand to indicate how close I was.

"Exactly how close is that?" my dad asked, knowing me so well.

"Dad, I have never been so close to close in my entire life."

"In other words, you're nowhere near done," he said.

"Progress is being made," I said, "but I'm going to need to stop in a while because I do have this other important meeting in the basement on my other assignment."

"Hank, the only meeting you're going to attend is the one where you introduce your butt to your desk chair, where it will remain until you're finished. Now go in your room and put your mind in gear."

When my dad gets in a mood like that, there's no arguing with him. I sighed loudly to see if I could make him feel bad. That didn't work, either. He didn't take his eyes off the TV. The sigh was a little for myself, too, because I knew that no matter how long I sat at my desk, I was never going to understand fractions. I have trouble with whole things, let alone bits and pieces of stuff.

I went back into my room and plopped down on my desk chair. After another minute of staring at the paper, I found myself opening my desk drawer and staring at the green plastic organizer I keep my supplies in. Oh, no! All my paper clips had moved from the round compartment where I keep them into the long compartment where I keep my pencils. I couldn't have that. I may not be a fast learner, but I like organization. It makes me feel good when my pencils are sharpened and my paper-clip holder is full and my rubber bands are all together in their plastic baggy.

"Hank," my mom said, opening the door a crack and sticking her head in.

Phew. I pushed the drawer closed just in time so she couldn't see that I wasn't concentrating. Actually, I was concentrating, just not on what I was supposed to be concentrating on. Why doesn't that count?

"Hey, Mom," I said. "What's up?"

"Dinner is up," she said. "And it's on the table."

"Please, Mom, I can't come to the table tonight. I only have a little while left to finish this math homework, and I have to meet Frankie and Ashley at seven."

"I'll bring your plate in here, honey," she said, which will tell you just how great a mom she is.

"Thanks, Mom. I really appreciate that."

She returned in a minute with a plate of brown rice and tofu with some broccoli trees mixed in.

"This will help you with your homework," she said. "Everything on that plate is brain food."

It certainly wasn't mouth and tongue food, I can tell you that. So now I had math problems I couldn't solve and food I couldn't eat. What else could possibly go wrong?

Clink. My digital clock now said six fifty-one.

The phone rang and I picked it up.

"Hey, Zip," Frankie said. "Ashweena and I are finished with our homework, so we're going down to the basement a little early. Can you meet us?"

"I'm almost done," I said. "I'll be there in five minutes."

I don't know why I just didn't tell Frankie the truth—that I was stuck on my math homework and making no progress. Actually, I do know why. Because I'm always the last to finish everything, and it gets really old being the slow one.

"Okay," Frankie said. "And don't be late. We lugged the books home, but you've got to do some of the research. It's only fair."

"Of course I'm going to be there," I said, wanting to bite my tongue before the words were even out of my mouth. "Research is my middle name."

"Really, dude? I thought your middle name was Daniel."

Ordinarily, I would have laughed at Frankie's little joke, but I was already starting to feel bad that I hadn't told him what was really happening.

"Hey, the longer we talk, the longer it's going to take me," I said to him. "So bye."

"See you in five, Zip."

I know what you're thinking. I still had nineteen more problems to go and only five minutes to do them in. I'd never be able to get them done.

And you know what? You're right.

CHAPTER 10

It was ten minutes after eight when I finally walked into our clubhouse in the basement. And you don't have to be a genius to realize right off the bat that Frankie and Ashley were angry. I mean, steam was coming out of every hole in their faces.

"We've been calling you, Zip," Frankie said.

"I know," I answered.

"You were supposed to be here an hour and ten minutes ago," Ashley said.

"I know."

"You were supposed to help with the research."

"I know."

"But now we've done it all, and you did exactly nothing. Nada. Zippo."

"I know, I know, I know. But I can explain."

"You know what, Zip," Frankie said, closing up the books that were open on the couch and standing up. "After a while, the explanations don't really matter. What matters is that we counted on you to be part of a team, and you weren't here, which means . . ."

"I know what it means," I said in frustration. "That you and Ashweena did all the work."

"Not to mention that we spent an hour in the library looking for just the right books," Ashley added. "Plus we had to convince the librarian that we could check out more than the limit, and then we carried a two-ton pile of books all the way here."

"And then you're a no-show," Frankie said, finishing me off entirely. "What kind of a team is that?"

"I think it's just a fraction of a team," I said, and for a second, I was very grateful to my math worksheet.

There was a lot of silence in our clubhouse. I looked around at all the shelves, loaded with cardboard boxes that people stored stuff in because there wasn't enough closet space in their apartment. I tried to read all the labels written on the boxes, just to stop thinking about how bad I felt. *Beach hats and towels. Vinyl records, 1968–1978. Grandma's quilts.* I wished I could throw one of Grandma's quilts over my head and disappear.

From down the hall, we could hear the washing machine in the laundry room groan to a halt. Somebody would be down soon to move their clothes into the dryer.

"Hey, I've got a great idea," I said, trying to make it sound like I really did have a great idea. "I'll go upstairs, get Cheerio, bring him down, and we can start teaching him a new trick right this second."

"I can't," Frankie said. "I have to go upstairs and finish my history note cards."

"And I promised my grandmother I would read her a chapter of this new book we're reading together," Ashley said.

I guess they could see my disappointment, because Frankie put his hand on my shoulder and looked me straight in the eye.

"When you're on a team, Zip, you make a commitment. You have to be there when it counts, when your team members are there.

Otherwise, you let people down."

"All of us know that Frankie and I can handle the research ourselves," Ashley added, "but that's not the point. If we make a commitment to do it together, that's the way it's got to be. Sorry, Hank. I have to go now."

She gathered up half the books, Frankie took the other half, and they hurried out the door. They walked down the hall to the elevator, and I stood in the clubhouse by myself.

All I could say was, "I know. I know."

But there was no one there to hear me.

CHAPTER 11

Most days, I have breakfast (whether I want to or not) with my sister Emily. I usually have cereal, because I like to construct things out of the cornflakes in my bowl before they get too soggy, like a bridge to Brooklyn or even the Empire State Building.

My sister Emily, on the other hand, doesn't build anything with her cereal. Instead, she reads science magazines and talks nonstop about the stuff she's reading. Like right in the middle of her Fruit Loops, she'll just start reading out loud about how the call of the humpback whale can be heard from over five hundred miles away. And then, if I dare to interrupt her with a question like, "How do they make the sound?" she'll say, "That's for us science lovers to know, and for you to look up."

So I wasn't too upset when Emily didn't show up for breakfast the next morning. My mom told me she had gone to school early to help the kindergarten teacher, Mrs. McMurray, clean out the hamster cages. Me, I wouldn't clean a hamster cage with *your* hands, let alone *my* hands. And if I was forced to do it, I'd wear at least fifteen pairs of rubber gloves and a gas mask.

My mom was getting dressed to go to her pregnant-lady exercise class, so it was just me and Cheerio in the kitchen. I thought I'd use the time to get in a little extra training with him. In between each bite of cereal, I tried to teach him to sit on his hind legs at attention. I was thinking that if I could get him to sit at attention, then I could teach him to salute with his front paw, and that trick would absolutely win him Mascot of the Year.

But Cheerio had other ideas.

"Sit up tall," I commanded him, holding my cereal spoon filled with cornflakes just above his nose.

He jumped up, grabbed the spoon out of my hand, and left the kitchen. When he came back, he had a cornflake stuck to his upper lip.

I got another spoon from the drawer, held it above his nose, and repeated the command.

"Concentrate, Cheerio. Now sit up tall."

Just then, the refrigerator started to hum. Even though he's heard that sound a million times, Cheerio stopped concentrating, ran to the refrigerator, and started barking at it like it was a robber.

"Cheerio!" I said. "You're never going to get the title unless you focus. What does it take to get you to settle down? Now come here and put your butt on the floor and your mind in gear."

Boy, was I ever sounding like my dad again.

Cheerio didn't care who I was sounding like. I hadn't even finished my sentence and he was on his way to the living room to roll on his back and scratch himself on the rug.

"Okay," I called to him. "If you want to be an underachiever, go right ahead."

Fine. If he didn't care that I was lecturing him like Stanley Zipzer, then I didn't care, either. I'd go right ahead and do it. Actually, it felt kind of good to let out all my frustration with him.

I got up and spent about five minutes

looking for my backpack, which I finally found in the hamper. I wondered how it got in there. Then I had to locate my fractions worksheet, and that was on the floor of my room, under my damp towel. That was good. I hoped that maybe some of my answers would smear, so Ms. Adolf couldn't tell they were all wrong. By the time I came back from my room, Cheerio was lying next to the potted plant in the living room, chewing on his favorite stuffed monkey.

"You have all day to relax," I said to him. "When I come home, we're going to have a really good training session with Frankie and Ashley. Let's show them that you can get down to business."

Cheerio tossed the monkey up in the air and growled. I decided to take that as a sign of agreement.

"Bye, Mom," I called out as I opened the front door. "Have a good exercise class. I hope the baby doesn't sweat."

"Thanks, honey," she yelled back. "Have fun in school."

Yeah, like that was going to happen.

Frankie and Ashley were waiting for me

outside our building. The mornings were still pretty nippy, and they looked cold. They were jumping up and down like they were trying to keep warm. Or like I do when I'm nervous and can't stand still.

"Sorry I'm late, guys," I said. "Cheerio and I were having a real heart-to-heart, and he promised that he was going to shift it into high gear and focus."

"Listen, dude," Frankie said, "about Cheerio . . ."

"We want to talk to you about him," Ashley chimed in. She looked weird, like she had just eaten a bad peanut.

"What's up?" I asked.

"We're going to make a change," Frankie said.

"Yeah," Ashley added. "A change about the mascot contest."

"Say no more," I said to them. "I am right with you on that. I was just telling Cheerio that there's going to be no more horsing around. It's a new day, and high time we get serious about this. So I've decided that this afternoon . . ."

"Zip, that's not the kind of change we had in mind."

Ashley took a deep breath. "Hank," she said. "We've decided that we're going over to Team Katherine."

"Katherine is Emily's pet," I said. "Katherine is competing *against* Cheerio. So you can't be on her team, because that would mean you'd be on two teams at once."

"We're not on two teams, Zip," Frankie said.

"Good, because you scared me there for a minute."

"We're only going to be on one team," Ashley said.

"Right. Team Cheerio. Just like we planned."

"Wrong," Frankie said. "Team Katherine. Just like we didn't plan."

"Wait a minute," I said. "Are you telling me that you're resigning from Team Cheerio?"

"See, it's like this," Ashley said, pushing her purple rhinestone glasses up on her nose. "Emily and Robert came by a little while ago. And they told us about their plans for Katherine. Did you know they're teaching to her walk backward while balancing a grape on her snout?"

"She'll never do that," I said. "She's a reptile. All they can do is stand in one place and hiss."

"Emily says she's learning, Zip. And when she does, she's going to blow all the other contestants out of the water. She'll win, and if we're on her team, we'll get our picture in the paper."

"Frankie. Listen to me. You'll get your picture in the paper when Cheerio wins!"

"Face it, Zip. Cheerio is never going to pay attention long enough to learn a trick, let alone two or three."

"And Emily and Robert have a whole training plan for Katherine," Ashley added. "They follow through, Hank. They already have most of the written report done. They always meet their responsibility."

"So that's what this is about?" I said. I could hear myself kind of yelling. "You're still mad at me about missing the meeting last night?"

"It's not just last night, Zip. Working with you means we'd have to do most of the work ourselves. And that's just not fun."

I took a deep breath to calm myself down.

"So let me get this straight," I said, after I had sucked in a whole ton of the morning air. "You're really and truly, one hundred percent, saying that you're quitting Team Cheerio?"

"That's pretty much it," Frankie said. "No hard feelings, buddy?"

"No," I said, not knowing what else to say. "Cheerio and I will do this by ourselves. We got it all locked up."

"Good luck," Ashley said. "We'll be friendly competitors, okay?"

"Sure," I said. "That's exactly what I was going to say."

But as we set out down 78th Street for school, my brain was saying something entirely different.

CHAPTER 12

(white flag)

Fort Coward

TEN THINGS MY BRAIN WAS SAYING AS I WALKED DOWN 78TH STREET

1. I can't believe they quit.
2. I can't believe they quit.
3. I can't believe they quit.
4. They quit. I can't believe it.
5. They actually quit. I can't believe it.
6. Can you believe it? They quit.
7. Wait a minute. They actually quit.
8. Holy mackerel, they quit!
9. Have I told you that they really did quit?
10. I can't believe they quit.

CHAPTER 13

As if the day hadn't started badly enough, Ms. Adolf gave us a pop quiz on fractions. There were ten problems and I got one correct. It was one half plus one half, which I know equals a whole. The fact that I knew that made me so excited I can't even explain it to you. Ms. Adolf didn't share my excitement, though. She wrote a big red F on the top of my quiz, which, by the way, did not stand for Fantastic or Fabulous or Far Out.

There it was. Another F.

You know, my father says I'm lazy. Ms. Adolf says that I need to focus. Even my mom, who really tries to understand my learning differences, says I would do a lot better if I just applied myself to my schoolwork. What do they think? That I want to fail? That I'm doing this on purpose? I lie in bed at night, and I think to myself, *Are you trying hard, Hank?* And I promise you, I am.

Sometimes I think tomorrow, I'm going to try harder. And then tomorrow comes and my brain still can't figure out fractions. Man, it's frustrating.

So you can imagine how glad I was when the bell rang for lunch and I could wipe all thoughts of math and fractions and Fs out of my head. I grabbed my brown bag, because it wasn't macaroni day, and headed for the lunchroom. By the time I got a milk and a dessert, Frankie and Ashley were already sitting at our usual table. What wasn't usual was that Robert and Emily were there, too. All four of them were in a deep discussion.

"Hey, guys," I said, sliding onto the bench next to Ashley. "This looks serious."

"We're having an important meeting, Hank," Emily said.

"About what?" I said with a laugh. "Iguana toenail clippings?"

"Actually, yes," Robert said. "Iguana grooming is the subject."

"And no offense, dude, but it's private," Frankie said.

"Oh," I said. "Okay. Don't mind me, I'll just sit here quietly."

I reached into my brown bag and took out the plastic baggy that contained my sandwich. Soylami again! I held my nose and was about to take a bite, when suddenly I realized the four of them were staring at me in silence.

"What?" I said. "I did not make this sandwich. Trust me."

"Hank," Ashley began, shifting her eyes away from me. "This is a meeting of Team Katherine. And it really is private."

"Meaning just us," Frankie said.

"Meaning beat it, big brother," Emily said.

"Why can't I just sit here and eat my lunch? It's not like I'm going to steal your lizard secrets or anything."

"You never know," Emily said. "Let me remind you that you are the competition."

"Okay, okay," I said, putting my sandwich back in its baggy. "I get it. Team Cheerio is leaving."

That reminded me that maybe I had

better find a Team Cheerio. One guy and one dachshund does not make a team.

Luke Whitman was sitting at a table by himself. That happens a lot to him. When you pick your nose during lunch, it cuts down on the number of people who can stomach sharing a table with you. Lucky for me, Luke's digging finger was on a break, so I slid onto the bench across from him.

"Luke! Just the guy I was looking for," I began. "How would you like to be a proud member of Team Cheerio and help me train the greatest dachshund in the city of New York."

"Sorry, Hank. I have another plan."

"What plan could be better than being part of a surefire winning team?"

"Can you keep a secret?" Luke whispered.

"Yeah."

"Don't tell anyone, but I'm training a garden slug to be the school mascot. His name is Fritz, and he lives in the flower box outside our living room window. I feed him already-been-chewed vegetables."

"Luke. Give me a break. No one is ever going

to choose a slug as the school mascot. Slugs are slimy and disgusting."

"Not Fritz. He is one good-looking slug. He oozes in all the right places."

With that, Luke's nose-picking finger shot into his nose. I thought it was a perfect time to leave.

Heather Payne was sitting at the next table, with two of her smart-girl friends. Even though Heather is the smartest and tallest person in the fifth grade, she and I have become friends since we were in the school play together. She would make a great member of Team Cheerio.

"Hi, Heather," I said. "Mind if I join you guys?"

"Of course not, Hank." She scooted over to make room for me next to her. "We were just talking about the best way to prepare note cards for the history research paper. I was suggesting pink cards for facts and blue cards for opinions."

"And white cards for neither," I said, chuckling at my own joke. I noticed that nobody else was. "White . . . as in blank cards. Get it?"

They still weren't laughing. In fact, they

weren't even smiling. Not a tooth was showing. The old Zipzer attitude sure wasn't in gear that day. And I can't tell you how hard I was looking for the ignition switch.

"So, Heather," I said, figuring that the best way with this crowd was to get right down to business. "I'm looking for a select few to join me on Team Cheerio."

"Gee, Hank, that's a really nice invitation," Heather responded. "But I don't have time because I've just started peer-tutoring Jeremy Ellington. Poor kid, he's having trouble with word problems."

"I can relate." I nodded. "But if anyone can help him, you can, Heather. You're a great tutor. Just don't tell him that there are fractions in his future, or he'll vomit on the spot."

The girls went back to discussing note card colors, and I got out of there fast. First of all, if I could actually take notes, I wouldn't care what color card they would be on. And second of all, I had work to do. The contest was Friday, exactly one week away, and so far, Team Cheerio consisted of just me.

I got up and looked around the lunchroom

to see if there was anyone else I could ask to join. My two best friends were deep in their team meeting without me. Luke was training a slug that looked like something he found in his nose. And me, where was I?

I'm on my way out of this cafeteria, that's where I am.

I actually ran out of the lunchroom and onto the playground. My head hurt. Where was I going to find a partner? What was I going to do?

"Hi, Hank," a little voice said. It was Mason Harris Jerome Dunn, my kindergarten buddy. "What'cha thinking about?"

I stared at Mason for a long time.

"Mason, my friend," I said, throwing my arm around his shoulder. "You're not going to believe this. I was just thinking about you!"

CHAPTER 14

We were over in the kindergarten area of the playground, where there's a sandbox and a jungle gym and a red plastic slide. Mason jumped into the sand, turned around so I couldn't see his face, and then suddenly spun around.

"Gggrrrrrrrrrrrrrrrrrrrrrrrrrrr," he said, lunging across the sand and putting his face right up next to mine.

"What are you doing, Mason?"

"I'm a T. rex," he said. "I'm growling. Gggrrrrrrrrrrrrrrrrrrrrrrr!"

He put his hands in front of his chest so they looked like little T. rex claws and pounced on me. I lost my balance and fell over into the sand. He pounced on me again, and growled right into my ear. My eardrum started to bang itself silly, like it was going to pop out of my ear and march in a parade.

"Ease up, little guy," I said.

"I'm not a little guy. I'm a T. rex," Mason reminded me.

"Right, T. rex. Back off, will you?"

"T. rexes don't back off. They attack. And they never give up. Ggggrrrrrrrrrrrr."

"Cool, Mason. That's the attitude I'm looking for. The never give up part, that is. Not the growling part."

"T. rex is hungry," Mason said. Just then, another kindergarten girl with bright red ribbons in her pigtails walked by. Mason jumped out at her, with his little claw hands pointed in her direction, and let loose another monster growl. She screamed.

"Stop doing that," she shouted as she ran off. "I'm telling Mrs. McMurray on you!"

Mason laughed, pretty satisfied with his little self.

"Come with me, buddy," I said, leading him by the hand over to an empty area of the sandbox.

I picked up one of the blue plastic shovels and used it to draw a square in the sand.

"Stand in there," I said to him.

"Why?" Mason wanted to know.

"Because it's T. rex Land," I said.

"Hank, it's just a stupid square."

"That's if you have no imagination. But my imagination says that whenever you stand in that square, you will turn into a T. rex and you can roar from now until the next Ice Age."

"Really?" Mason said. I could see his little eyes light up.

"Yeah, and when you're with your friends, you don't have to scare them. You can save all your scary stuff for Dinosaur Land."

That made Mason really happy. He stood in that square and let out five or six powerful roars.

"Okay, I'm done for now," he said. "Let's play something else."

"That's exactly what I wanted to talk to you about, Mason. I have a great game. It's called Let's Teach Cheerio a Trick."

"How can you teach a piece of cereal a trick?" he asked. "Oh, I know. You mean like floating on its back in milk."

"Wrong Cheerio, Mase. I'm talking about my dog. Remember him?"

"Oh yeah. The little wiener dog. He's short and funny."

"Just like you."

"I'm not short. I'm five."

"Good point," I said. "So are you in?"

"Okay, I'll play," Mason agreed. "Can we start now?"

"You have to go back to class now. We can start later."

"I don't want to go back to class," Mason sulked, "because it's alphabet time and I hate the alphabet. I can't keep all those letters in order in my brain."

"I know exactly how you feel," I said. "But here's the deal. We can't get going until after school. Then we'll take Cheerio to the park and start teaching him."

"Can my mom come? Because it's Tuesday and that's our park day."

"Sure, she can come. See how perfect this is working out, Mase? Finally, Team Cheerio is moving full steam ahead."

I know what you're thinking. Recruiting one five-year-old who thinks he's a T. rex is not exactly full steam ahead. But I was determined to make the best of this. Like my mom always says, if life gives you a lemon, make lemonade. Just be sure to leave out the white sugar because it's very bad for your dental health.

Just at the moment when I was finally starting to feel better about Team Cheerio and my hopes for the mascot contest, who walked by but Nick the Tick. I could hear his big lumbering feet pounding the playground as he stomped up to us. He was the real T. rex.

"You're pathetic, Zipperbutt," he said. "Hanging out with a kindergartner."

"I'm on Team Cheerio," Mason said to him, putting his hands on his hips.

McKelty laughed, spitting out a few chocolate crumbs that were left over in his teeth from lunch.

"What is he?" McKelty said to me. "The pet you're entering?"

"Very classy, McKelty," I said. "Picking on little kids takes a lot of guts. Why don't you wander off and steal somebody's lunch."

"Hey, I'm glad I thought of that," the big oaf said. "I'm still really hungry."

With that, he left to go rummage through the

trash can and find someone's leftover dessert.

"I don't like him," Mason said.

"Don't worry about it, buddy. We're going to show him. Just wait until Team Cheerio struts its stuff. Guys like him are going to wish they were us."

Boy, oh boy. I wished I believed that.

CHAPTER 15

Holy mackerel! By the time we got to Riverside Park, there was hardly any room left on the grass area to train Cheerio on.

In one section, over by the chain-link fence that separates the basketball courts from the rest of the park, Nick McKelty was working with his annoying little Chihuahua, Fang. He was actually trying to teach his dog how to ride his bicycle. Fang's legs were about as long as a human thumb, and if you know anything about thumbs, you know that they can't reach the pedals on a two-wheeler. I guess old McKelty hadn't figured that out yet.

In another section, Ryan Shimozato and his crew were working with his dog, a Great Dane who looked like a small horse. Correction, make that a big horse. They were trying to teach him to roll over, but he seemed to prefer sniffing under the park benches for old chewing gum. It took all four guys on Ryan's team pulling on his leash to get that horse-dog away from the bench slats.

And taking up all the concrete space in the middle of the park area was none other than my little sister Emily and her posse, which consisted of Robert, and my two supposed-to-be best friends, Frankie and Ashley. Or as I like to call them, traitors.

They had Katherine on a homemade leash, which I very soon recognized as the belt I wore to my Aunt Maxine's birthday party. They were gathered around Katherine, trying to coax her to walk backward while balancing a grape on her snout. I don't mean to sound bitter, but there it was. The grape actually *was* on the tip of her snout.

How did they teach her to do that? Katherine's a reptile, for goodness sake. With a brain the size of two mashed peas.

Mason, his mom, and I walked past the concrete area to look for a place suitable for Cheerio's lesson. I was planning to ignore Team Katherine so I could look like I didn't care for one minute that the sack of scales was doing the most amazing trick ever. But when Cheerio saw Emily, he bolted from my hands, charged up, and started licking her knees, which is the only thing he could reach. Mason ran after Cheerio, but stopped suddenly when he came face-to-face with a hissing Katherine.

"You are ugly," he said, right to Katherine's face. Then he growled his biggest T. rex roar right at her.

Katherine, who didn't know that kindergarteners like to pretend to be dinosaurs, wasn't phased by his growling. She opened her iguana mouth, showed him every one of her 188 teeth, and hissed up a storm. Mason screamed, flew into a backward somersault, raced for his mom, and grabbed her hand.

"Don't be scared, Mase," I told him. "Katherine's all hiss and no bite."

"I'm not scared," he said. "I just wanted to make sure my mom was still here."

"Hank," Emily said. "Team Katherine is really working hard here. So could you just stay over there in your own work area?"

"No problem," I said, "because Team

Cheerio isn't interested in showing you what's in our bag of tricks."

"Zip, it's not like we don't know what Team Cheerio is trying to accomplish," Frankie said. "We were just on it yesterday."

"Oh, that's where I know you from," I said.

"Hank, don't be that way," Ashley pleaded. "This is about the animals, not us."

"Fine," I answered. "You play with your animal, if you can call it that, and I'll play with mine. Come on, Mase. You can let your mom go now."

We set up our training area in a grassy spot by the path along the river. Mason's mom took a seat on a nearby bench and started to knit a green and yellow baby hat.

"Okay, Mason. I'll give Cheerio the command and you stand over there with a treat in your hand. Every time he follows the command, you give him a piece of soylami from the baggy."

"Can I have some, too, if I do something good?"

"Sure, Mase. Knock yourself out."

He opened the baggy and took a sniff.

"That's okay," he said under his breath. "I'll wait for dinner."

I took Cheerio off his leash. "Okay, Cheerio. Time to focus. You can do this, I know you can. Now, sit up on your hind legs."

I raised my hand in the air, so he could follow it with his eyes.

"Up, boy. Come on. Up."

I swear to you, he was just about to do it. I could see it in his eyes. They had a real sitting-up kind of look. But before he could actually do it, a bicycle came whizzing along the path next to us. McKelty was holding the seat, thumping along next to it, while his Chihuahua was using all four paws to hold on to the seat for dear life. The look on that little dog's face said, "Please, someone! Anyone! Get me off this thing, and quick!"

All of a sudden, Fang let out a squeal, and I really think I heard him say, "Ayyyyyy, caramba!"

Cheerio heard it, too, because in a flash, he was off and running, chasing McKelty's bike and nipping at the rubber back wheel.

"Hey, get your wiener dog out of here,"

McKelty hollered. "Get control of him."

Easier said than done. Cheerio kept nipping at the wheel, then at McKelty's pant leg. McKelty, who is not exactly coordinated to begin with, tripped over his own big feet, and went sprawling onto the path. The bike went down on top of him, and Fang went flying. Luckily, he made a soft landing on McKelty's face. He was safe except for the bad breath that was gushing out of McKelty's mouth. I bet that blast of toxic breath made the poor little guy wish he was back on the bicycle, even though he had been scared out of his wits.

"Everyone okay here?" a voice said.

It was Officer Quinn, doing his rounds along the park path. He bent over and lifted Fang off McKelty's face, then helped McKelty up.

"No, I am definitely not okay," McKelty whined. "This little wiener dog attacked my bicycle wheel. Isn't there a law against that?"

"Hank, you know better than this," Officer Quinn said to me. "Your dog is supposed to be on a leash."

"What about his?" I said. "His was riding a bicycle."

"No kidding," Officer Quinn said. "That's a pretty good trick."

"My dog is a real champion," McKelty bragged. "His father was the official Chihuahua to the emperor of Mexico."

There it was again, in full action—the McKelty Factor.

"Hank, look," Mason called out. "Cheerio's doing it."

Sure enough, there was Cheerio on the grassy area, sitting on his hind legs, waving with his right paw.

"I'm going to give him a treat," Mason said.

Mason opened the baggy to get out a chunk of soylami. Unfortunately, my mom's soylami has a powerful odor, which made its way over to Ryan Shimozato's Great Dane's nose. Before you could say "whoa, boy," that horse-dog took off across the grass, pulling Ryan and his posse like they were riding a sled through the winter snow. The Great Dane snatched the entire baggy from Mason's hands, and in one swipe of his humongous tongue, the soylami and the baggy disappeared down his throat.

The commotion was too much for Katherine, who is used to the peace and quiet and boredom of Emily's room. She let out a hiss that sounded like the air going out of a truck tire, and took off across the concrete. When she reached the first tree, she climbed up the trunk, and hung onto the bark with her nine-inch claws. My belt was still hanging off her neck, but she was too far up the tree for Emily to grab it. Katherine was so nervous that she just clung there, hissing and staring at the sky.

"Now look what you've done," Emily shouted at me. "Katherine is having a panic attack."

"How can you tell?" I shot back at her. "To me, it just looks like an ugly attack."

"That's not funny, Hank. Our entire training session is ruined because of you."

"If we're really lucky, she'll stay in that tree for the next six years."

"Yeah, this whole mess is all your wiener dog's fault," McKelty said. "He's a menace to society."

"Hey, look!" Mason shouted. "Cheerio's rolling over. He's really smart. Now he's sitting up. Now he's rolling over again."

Cheerio must have given the Great Dane the idea, because suddenly he started rolling over and over in the grass. He looked like a blue whale, which is supposed to be the largest mammal on earth. As he rolled on the grass, he came dangerously close to Fang, who didn't stand a chance if that Great Dane decided to roll over on him.

"Okay, okay!" Officer Quinn said, trying to capture Fang to get him out of the way. "Everyone put your animals on a leash. This has gotten way out of hand."

"Don't blame my fabulously talented dog," McKelty said. "It's all the wiener dog's fault. He's the one who took off after my dog."

Cheerio didn't like the sound of that at all, and I can't blame him. McKelty's been insulting me ever since I've been in preschool, and sometimes you want to really go after that big bully. Which is exactly what Cheerio did. He lowered his whole body, which was already pretty darn low, into the grass, and stalked McKelty like a lion stalking his prey.

"Don't do it, Cheerio," I warned. "This is not the time or place."

Cheerio looked at me, then looked at Officer Quinn. I could tell he was trying to figure out what his chances were.

"You wouldn't dare, short stuff," McKelty said to him.

Uh-oh. The one thing you don't want to do is to call my dachshund short. He's very sensitive on the subject.

Cheerio leaped into the air like SuperDog and landed right on McKelty's shin.

"Protect me, Fang," McKelty said.

Fang, brave protector that he was, immediately jumped onto Officer Quinn's shoe, raised his hind leg, and let loose a yellow river. Or maybe, since he was just a tiny Chihuahua, you'd call it more of a stream.

That did it. Officer Quinn had one very wet shoe and that seemed to make him angry. Cheerio just stood in front of Fang, barking at him like a maniac. If you could understand dog talk, I'll bet you would have heard him saying, "Don't call me short, shortie!" But if you didn't understand dog talk, it just sounded like Cheerio had gone nuts.

Officer Quinn reached down and picked up Cheerio, who immediately licked his face, trying to make nice.

It didn't work.

"You've caused a lot of trouble here," he said to Cheerio. "And now you've got to come with me down to the police station."

I couldn't believe it!

"You're arresting him?"

"I have to take him in, Hank. Disorderly canine conduct."

"But, he didn't mean to do anything bad. He just has trouble focusing. And following directions."

"Yeah," Frankie chimed in. "Underneath, he's really a good dog."

"Who tries really hard," Ashley agreed.

Oh, now they're defending Cheerio. Where were they when it mattered? Like this morning.

"I say take him in," McKelty said. "We're all safer with that mutt off the streets."

Mason jumped in front of McKelty with his hands in the T. rex attack position.

"Grrrrrrrrrrrrr," he roared in his fiercest,

loudest voice.

"I'm not scared of you, kid," McKelty said. "Go play with your mommy."

"That's an excellent idea," Mason's mom said, taking Mason by the hand. "I don't want him around a bad-mannered boy like you."

As Mason and his mom left the park, I reached out and gave Cheerio a pet. Poor guy, he didn't even know he had caused any trouble.

"I wish you were coming home with me, Cheerio," I said to him gently.

"I'm sorry, kid," Officer Quinn said to me. "Your dog's got to come with me to the station."

He held Cheerio in his arms, turned, and walked out of the park.

All I could do was follow him.

CHAPTER 16

Oh, no!

My mind was racing.

My little Cheerio. My puppy. My pet. My pal. My doggy vacuum cleaner.

In jail?

What was going to happen to him? Would he be sentenced to life behind bars? Would he have to eat prison meals? Well, it's got to be better than my mom's food. But still, he'd be locked up! When were visiting hours? Would they let him have his little navy blue terry-cloth bed? Or his squeaky kangaroo?

Oh, Cheerio. I have to help you.

CHAPTER 17

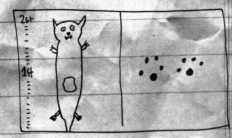

I couldn't let Cheerio out of my sight, so I followed very closely behind Officer Quinn. I didn't think he even knew I was there until we got to the station, when he held the door open for me so I could go in first.

"I have a great idea," I said, before I went into the station. "Why don't I just take Cheerio home so you can get on with the business of protecting and serving."

"I'm sorry, young man," Officer Quinn said. "A complaint has been filed by one of our citizens."

"Wait. You're calling Nick McKelty a citizen? Of what? The United States of Bullies?"

Officer Quinn didn't answer. He just went inside the station, put Cheerio down on the top of a counter, and asked the officer sitting behind the desk to help him start the booking process.

"The booking process?" I said, following Officer Quinn to the counter. "You mean Cheerio is a criminal?"

"Don't panic, kid," said the officer behind the desk. She had a blond ponytail and was chewing a big wad of bubble gum. "Fingerprinting him, or in his case, pawprinting him, just gives us a record of who's been in here."

I looked at the desk officer and pleaded with her.

"Please, Officer . . . Kras . . . Kras . . . Krascoz . . . I'm sorry I can't make out all those letters on your name badge. I'm not such a great reader."

"That's all right, sweetie," she said. "A lot of people have trouble with my name. Why don't you just call me Officer K and we'll leave it at that."

"Thank you so much, Officer K."

She was really nice. I think Cheerio liked her, too. I could tell because he jumped off the counter and into her lap and started licking her cheek. Or maybe he just liked the smell of her bubble gum. He is a sucker for anything watermelon-flavored.

"Whoa there, little guy," she said. "I can't socialize with the suspects."

"Officer K, please hand the dog over to me," Officer Quinn said.

Officer Quinn opened up an ink pad. He took Cheerio in his arms, held his front paw, and rolled it across the inky surface. I was watching Cheerio very carefully and I could see him getting agitated. He let out a low growl and his upper lip curled into a snarl.

"Don't even think about it, boy," I whispered to him. "You better be on your best behavior. And I mean it."

Cheerio settled down and let Officer Quinn press his inky paw on a sheet of paper. He didn't make a move when they did his other front paw, either. As a matter of fact, his curled lip had relaxed. I guess he was getting used to being in jail.

Or at least, that's what I thought. But was I ever wrong.

That whole time, he was just waiting for his opportunity to make a break. As soon as Officer Quinn turned his back, Cheerio leaped off the counter and took off running through the

105

station house. It wasn't hard to find him, though, because everywhere he went, he left two big black paw prints on the mint-green linoleum floor. When we finally caught him, he had jumped into a wastebasket next to the water cooler. I figured that out because the paw prints stopped right there.

"Cheerio, get out of that wastebasket," I commanded him. "You're just making things worse."

He didn't listen. He tried to burrow into the crumpled-up papers and empty coffee cups.

"You can't hide from the law, pup," Officer Quinn said. He was laughing by this time, which shows you that basically he is a really nice guy.

Cheerio peeked out from over the top of the wastebasket. His long ears flopped over the side, and all you could see were his big brown eyes and his black wet nose.

"Aww," said Officer K. "How could such a cute fellow like you cause so much trouble?"

Officer Quinn reached in and lifted Cheerio from the wastebasket.

"Excuse me, Officer," I said, "but doesn't he get to make one phone call?"

"Your dog is talented enough to dial the phone?"

"No, I was going to do it for him."

"Here, sweetie," Officer K said. "You can use my phone."

I went over to her desk and picked up the receiver. As much I didn't want to do it, I knew I had to call my dad. Cheerio was in trouble, which meant I was in trouble. We needed my dad, and that's all there was to it.

I started to dial our number, when suddenly, my mind went totally blank.

Oh come on, Hank. This is nuts. Who forgets their own phone number? I do, that's who. I know it like I know my name, but where is it? It's like it's playing hide-and-seek in my brain. This is no time for games! Come out, come out, wherever you are.

I took a breath and went with my best guess. The phone was ringing, and it sounded like our ring. That was good.

"Hello. Baja Fresh," the voice said on the other end of the phone.

That was bad.

"Hello. Uh . . . Stanley Zipzer isn't there by

any chance, is he? Maybe ordering a beef-and-cheese burrito?"

The guy on the other end of the phone must have covered the mouthpiece because I could hear his muffled yell.

"Anybody here named Stanley? With the last name of Zipzer? Sorry, kid. There's a Jimmy and a Salvador here. Salvador's got the taco grande. Does that sound like somebody you know?"

"No, sir, sorry. But I hope he enjoys his meal."

I hung up the phone and almost started to cry. That was our one call, and my stupid brain blew it. It's just like my brain to give up when I need it the most.

I looked at Cheerio. He seemed to be enjoying the delicious smell of Officer K's watermelon gum.

That's just great, I thought. *He's sniffing up a storm and having a fine old time. He doesn't even have a clue.*

But me, I know the truth.

We're going to be locked in here forever.

CHAPTER 18

Ten seconds later, the doors to the station burst open as if they were propelled by a super-human force, and my father, Stanley Zipzer, stormed through them with his finger pointed directly in between my eyes.

Let me just say from previous experience, I knew at that moment I was toast . . . burnt to a crisp.

"You," he said with his pointer finger getting closer and closer to my forehead, "need to start an explanation, and it had better be specific and convincing. Go!"

Okay, there it was. I knew exactly what I had to do, which, by the way, was a lot easier than the actual doing of it.

I figured out that after the chaos in the park, Frankie and Ashley and Emily and Robert probably ran home to get my dad and tell him

Cheerio and I were in trouble. I couldn't blame them for doing that. I mean, after all, we were in the police station, which is like a major step up from Principal Love's office.

Part of me was glad to see my dad. And the other part could've done without him being there.

I took a deep breath and felt all that good oxygen flood my brain. Finally I could start to think a little, and I noticed Frankie and Ashley trailing behind my dad.

"Dad. Let me just ask that you don't say one word until I finish the whole story," I began.

"You have no bargaining position here, young man, and I will speak whenever I have something to say."

"Deal. We'll play by your rules."

Before I could get one word out, Cheerio, who had finished posing for his mug shots, jumped off the stool and ran over to my dad. He sat down at his feet, put on his cutest face, looked my dad right in his not-so-cute face, and started to whimper like when he was a puppy.

"Don't you even try, mister," my dad said to him, wagging his pointer finger at Cheerio's snout. "You can't butter me up. I am hopping mad."

Officer K got up from her desk, walked over to Cheerio, and picked him up. He put his nose up to her mouth and took another whiff of the gum. His tail started to wag.

"I'll watch the dog while you two have your conversation," she said. "Sounds like you have a lot to work out."

"Thanks, Officer K," I said, hoping to impress my dad with what good manners I was displaying. He wasn't impressed.

"Ready, begin," he said. "And I mean now."

"So listen, Dad," I stammered. "You know how I have learning challenges and it's really difficult for me to focus sometimes."

"Oh, that again," my dad said. "I thought we had dealt with that."

"Maybe you did," I said. "But I'm sorry to tell you, Dad, my brain didn't. I keep trying to explain to you that it doesn't just go away."

"And what does all that learning challenges business have to do with you being here in the police station?"

"I'm thinking that some of those things I

have a hard time with—like paying attention and following directions and stuff—fell right out of my body and into Cheerio's. No matter what I tried at the park, he would get distracted by everything and cause trouble."

"Which is why I had to bring him here," Officer Quinn piped up. "I hated to do it, but your elongated dog racked up quite a list of complaints and almost caused bodily harm."

My dad shot Cheerio a disapproving look. Cheerio kind of cocked his head to the side, as if to say, "Don't blame me, I couldn't help it."

"I was there, Mr. Z," Frankie said. "And it really wasn't Hank's fault. He was trying his hardest."

"And Cheerio didn't even try to cooperate," Ashley added.

"Listen, kids. I know you're concerned about your friend," my dad said. "But this is between me and Hank."

That certainly zipped their lips. When my dad's in one of his fact-finding moods, nothing can get in the way of what he needs to know.

"Officer Quinn," my dad said, turning to him. "I apologize for my son's bad behavior and irresponsibility. But if you'll let him and the dog go, I promise you that I'll handle this matter at home."

"I won't press charges," Officer Quinn said, "if I see that they're going to learn something from this."

"Oh, trust me, he'll learn," my dad said. "He'll learn to love his bedroom, because that's where he's going to be until I decide it's time for him to come out. And allow me to say, Hank, that decision will not be made anytime soon."

"If I could suggest another alternative," Officer Quinn said. "We have a community service program that we find is very effective in dealing with young people in situations like this."

"Watch out, dude," Frankie whispered. "I see some trash-picking-up duty in your future."

He laughed but I didn't. He stopped immediately.

"Sorry," he said. "Inappropriate."

"As I was saying," Officer Quinn went on. "There is a senior center on 85th between Broadway and Amsterdam. And I'm sure some of the seniors would be delighted to have a visit from an energetic young man such as yourself,

Hank. You would put a smile on their face."

"Can Cheerio come, too?" I asked. "He relates well to older people."

"If you assure me that you can keep his behavior in check, that sounds like a good idea," Officer Quinn said.

"He needs community service, too. Maybe even more than you."

"I'll have him at the senior center starting tomorrow," my dad said.

"And every afternoon for the next two weeks," Office Quinn said.

"That doesn't include weekends, does it?" I asked.

"It most certainly does."

My father turned to face me.

"So, Hank," he stated. "Just know that for the next fourteen days, you can breathe, eat, sleep, go to school, and do your community service with full commitment."

If you looked up "grounded" in the dictionary, you couldn't find a more complete definition.

And there you had it. My life, or lack thereof, by Hank Zipzer.

CHAPTER 19

NINE THINGS CHEERIO DID AT THE SENIOR CENTER THAT I WISH HE HADN'T (AND SO DID THEY!)

1. He got his leash wrapped around Fern Bristol's wheelchair and pulled her down the hall on a thrill ride. Her mouth was open but she was so scared nothing came out except her teeth.

2. He knocked over Mr. Parkins's and Mr. Adelman's chess game and ate a rook. Actually, he ate two rooks but he was stopped before he could start on the queen.

3. He joined in during their sing-along, howling away at "This Land is Your Land" until everyone stopped but Cheerio, who thought they had given him a solo.

4. He stuck his snout in Mr. Davis's trombone, and when Mr. Davis blew a high note, Cheerio's long floppy ears shot straight up to the ceiling.

5. He got into the kitchen and ate 183 cups of applesauce and four chocolate puddings, and burped for the rest of the afternoon. Mrs. Carew kept asking, "Are we in an orchard?"

6. He snatched Mr. Hudnut's straw hat and peed on it so much the straw got all soggy and I spent the next half hour airing it out with a hair dryer.

7. He wouldn't stop licking Mrs. Chow's elbows because she uses a lotion that is scented with coconuts. She told him, "Beat it, pal. You're barking up the wrong tree."

8. He got into the art supplies, and let's just say, the art room at the senior center is now a red room.

9. He tried to play with a goldfish in the aquarium and scared that poor fish so much, it jumped out of its tank and down Mrs. Witt's blouse. It was never found again.

CHAPTER 20

ONE THING CHEERIO DID AT THE
SENIOR CENTER THAT I'M GLAD HE DID

1. He sat in every single person's lap and
   brought a smile to each of their faces.

CHAPTER 21

Papa Pete always says that there's a good side and a bad side to everything.

On the good side, working at the senior center made me feel great. I never knew seniors could be so much fun.

But on the bad side, working at the senior center took up every afternoon and all my free time. By the time I had dinner and finished my homework, there was not one second left to train Cheerio, which turned out not to matter because my dad forbid me to be in the mascot contest, anyway. He said that would teach me a life lesson in learning responsibility, although I personally don't get how *not* doing something teaches you responsibility. Seems to me like the lesson is "don't do things you really care about." But then, I've never claimed to understand what goes on inside the mind of Stanley Zipzer.

I waited a couple of days to see if he would change his mind, but when he didn't, I couldn't put it off anymore. On Tuesday, three days before the contest, I went up to Ms. Adolf after class and broke the sad news to her.

"Ms. Adolf," I began. I confess that my lower lip was trembling a little, which it does when I'm trying really hard not to cry. "I have to pull my dog Cheerio out of the mascot competition."

She was at her desk, busy locking up her top drawer with the grey key she wears around her grey neck. She barely looked up and didn't seem to share any of my disappointment.

"I think you've made the right decision, Henry," she said. "You shouldn't be wasting your time with that unruly dog, but rather applying yourself to the study of fractions."

At that moment, Nick McKelty was walking by on his way to recess, and of course, his big ears heard everything.

"Don't worry about it, Zipperbutt. That ugly mutt of yours would have come in last, anyway. He didn't have a chance."

"Butt out, McKelty. This is between me and Ms. Adolf."

"I'm just saying that your dog is a loser, like you."

"That will be enough, Mr. McKelty," Ms. Adolf scolded.

"Fine, I was finished, anyway." Then the jerk lumbered away, satisfied that his big mouth had done its job.

I could feel my lower lip tremble big-time now, and my blood boil.

"Excuse me, Ms. Adolf," said a voice from behind me. I didn't even have to turn around because I knew it was Frankie. "Ashley and I would like to enter a dog in the mascot competition."

"And what is your canine's name?" she asked.

"That would be Cheerio," Frankie said.

"What are you talking about?" I said to Frankie. "I just withdrew him."

"We heard," Frankie said. "So Ashley and I would like to take over Team Cheerio, if that's okay with you."

"Yeah . . . sure . . . but . . . wait a minute . . . you guys are . . . I mean . . . you left . . . and now you're here . . . and wow, I'm confused."

"Katherine doesn't need us," Ashley told me. "She's doing just fine. But you and Cheerio do."

"Besides," Frankie said. "We can't let McKelty get away with that attitude. Somebody's got to shut him down. And we think Cheerio's just the dog to do it."

Ms. Adolf was drumming her fingers impatiently on her desktop.

"Will one of you please tell me . . . is this animal in or out?" she said in a voice that sounded like she was remembering the last time she and Cheerio got tangled up. She was definitely not president of the Cheerio fan club.

"He's in," all three of us said together.

With that, I threw my arms around Frankie and Ashley, and as we headed out the door for recess, all I could think was how great it was to have friends like them.

CHAPTER 22

I was glad that Frankie and Ashley volunteered to train Cheerio, but there was one big problem, and it was my usual problem. Stanley Zipzer.

"So, Hank," my dad said at dinner as we were all trying to gag down my mom's newest creation, a meatless medley of grains and legumes from Cameroon that were mashed together to make them look like crab cakes. We weren't fooled, though. Those suckers were evil. I swear there was a dash of well-worn gym sock in there somewhere.

I didn't like the sound of my dad's "So, Hank." With him, nothing good ever follows "So, Hank."

"So, Hank," he repeated, just for emphasis. "Mrs. Aguilar, the director of the senior center, called this afternoon."

"Oh, you mean Delores," I said. "She's really nice. She let me Xerox both my palms on the big machine in her office. And in color, no less."

"Let me remind you that you're there to do community service, not to be fooling around copying your body parts."

"Just be grateful it was only his hands, Dad," Emily-the-helpful piped up. "Once he tried to Xerox his butt on the machine in the attendance office, but Ms. Crock caught him just before he pushed the start button."

"Thanks for supplying that information, Emily," I said. "I'll be sure to tell Dad about the time you . . ."

I stopped dead in my tracks. The truth was, I couldn't think of a time that she had ever done anything wrong. Wow, what a boring life she leads.

"So, Hank, back to the subject at hand," my dad said. "Mrs. Aguilar asked if you could be there at three-thirty tomorrow, rather than four. It seems there's a sing-along and she'd like you to make copies of the song sheets. I could bring Cheerio to meet you at three-thirty."

"I'm glad you brought this up, Dad," I said

as my mom came in carrying a platter of seconds of the phony crab cakes. I don't know why she felt that was necessary, because no one finished the first helping.

"I was thinking that Cheerio has done so well and really learned his lesson that he should be excused from any further community service," I said.

"Oh, Cheerio, I'm so proud of you," my mom said, throwing him one of the crab cakes, which he caught like a Frisbee in midair. That dog will eat anything. Doesn't he taste that hint of used gym sock at all?

"I know what you're thinking, Dad," I continued before my father could say anything. "This is not me trying to talk my way out of anything. I still have lessons to learn, and I would like to do community service for both of us."

If you're wondering if I had lost my marbles completely, I assure you I hadn't. My goal was to get Cheerio free in the afternoons, so Frankie and Ashley could continue his training in the park. There were only a two days left before the competition, and Cheerio had a lot of catch-up to do. That reminded me that I had to call

Mason to tell him he was back on the team. I told Frankie and Ashley that there was no way we could disappoint my little micro-buddy, and they agreed.

"I think Hank has a good point," my mom said. "From what I hear, Cheerio has brought a lot of joy to the seniors. They couldn't stop talking about him when I was there yesterday."

My mom had come to pick us up the day before and brought soylami and soystrami sandwiches for the seniors. They actually liked them. I guess when you get older, your tongue stops working.

"It was really mostly Hank's fault to begin with," Emily said, always happy to hurl an insult in my direction.

For once, I didn't defend myself and kept my mouth shut. Emily's argument was actually helping my case.

"I suppose I don't have any objection to suspending Cheerio's punishment," my dad said. "But it's a different story with you, young man."

"When you're right, you're right, Dad. And let me just say, you are righter than right."

Yay. I had what I wanted.

I couldn't wait to call Frankie and Ashley and tell them that Cheerio was cleared for training. I jumped up from the table, asked to be excused, and pushed my chair in, all in one quick motion.

"Dad," Emily whined. "He can't leave yet. I was just about to show everyone Katherine's new trick that is sure to win her the mascot contest."

"No offense, Em, but I have important things to do."

"Da-aa-aaad," Emily whined.

"Sit down, Hank," my mom said. "We're a family and your sister has something to share."

"That lizard does not live in my family tree," I said.

"Katherine is as much a part of our family as Cheerio is," my mom said. "Just like Ralph was."

Oh, man. She had to go and bring up Ralph, my pet turtle when I was four who disappeared when I was taking him for a walk down Broadway. I'm pretty positive he's living a happy life in the sewer. But I couldn't argue with my mom when she played the Ralph card.

I turned to face the ugly lizard.

"Okay, Kathy. Show us what you got. But please, hurry up. I have an important phone call to make."

Part of the reason I didn't want to see Katherine's trick was that I suspected she had something really good up her sleeve and I didn't want to get discouraged about Cheerio's lack of progress.

But nothing could have prepared me for what I saw.

Emily took Katherine from around her neck, where she had been wearing her like a scarf, and put her on the dining room table. She held her hand above Katherine's head, and Katherine followed her until her snout was facing the ceiling. Then Emily took a grape out of her pocket and balanced it on the tip of Katherine's snout. When the grape was very steady, Emily took a baton out of her pocket. Well, it wasn't a real baton, but one that she made out of a Q-tip and tin foil. She placed the baton on top of the grape.

And if that wasn't enough, that reptile started walking backward, balancing the grape and the baton on top of her snout.

My mouth fell open so wide, I had to actually take my hand and push my lower jaw back up.

I looked over at Cheerio, who was finishing the last bit of his second phony crab cake, and thought, *You better enjoy that while it lasts, pal, because you really got your work cut out for you.*

CHAPTER 23

For the next two days, I went to the senior center and did my community service, which, I have to say, was actually pretty fun. There is something about helping people and putting a smile on their faces that makes you feel really good, even if you are missing your dog's most important two training sessions of his life.

In the evening, Frankie, Ashley, and I met in our basement clubhouse to review Cheerio's progress. Here is a summary of what they told me.

FIVE THINGS CHEERIO ALMOST LEARNED

1. He *almost* learned to roll over, but stopped midway on his back and insisted on waving

all four of his feet to air them out.

2. He *almost* learned to sit up on his hind legs, but kept falling over because his top part is longer than his bottom part.

3. He *almost* learned to snatch a Frisbee out of the air, but every time he was about to catch it, he'd just sit down and lick his tail.

4. He *almost* learned to walk with his head held high on a leash, but instead he grabbed the leash in his teeth and pulled Mason into the birdbath, at which time the training was over because Mason's mom took him right home to change his clothes so he wouldn't catch a cold. (You can only imagine the steam coming out of Mason's mom's ears.)

5. Ashley made him a rhinestone crown that he *almost* learned to wear, but instead he shook it off his head, grabbed it in his mouth, ran to the bank of the Hudson, and flung it in the river. (I have to say, I'm on Cheerio's side on this one. Come on, he's not a rhinestone kind of guy.)

By the time the week was over, Cheerio was

as ready as he was ever going to be for the competition, which . . . let's face it . . . was not ready at all.

CHAPTER 24

On the day of the mascot competition, all of the kids at PS 87 gathered on the bleachers that lined the walls of the multipurpose room. Those who had entered a pet in the competition sat in a row of chairs on the stage that were placed on either side of the judges' table.

The judges included Ms. Adolf, who wore (you guessed it) a grey pantsuit. At least, I think it was a pantsuit. I couldn't tell where the pants ended and the jacket started. Sitting next to her was her monster boxer, Randolf Bartholomew Irving Adolf. We all hoped that he had skipped breakfast, and the previous night's dinner for that matter, too. (If you remember, the digestive rumblings that came out of that dog could curl your nose hairs and make your socks go up and down.) Randolf was wearing a starched white collar with a grey bowtie. I guess his favorite color had to be grey, too, if he was going to live in her house.

The other judge was the kindergarten teacher, Mrs. McMurray. Frankie, Ashley, and I figured they picked her because when you're a kindergarten teacher dealing with a roomful of five-year-olds, it's like trying to control a basket full of puppies, anyway. She had really gotten herself into the spirit of the day. She was wearing a sweater with pink and red cats and dangling earrings that were fish—I think they were trout, but I'm not an expert on types of fish. And on her skirt, there was a fluffy white poodle with rhinestone eyes.

"Now that's my kind of skirt," Ashley whispered to me as we led Cheerio to his chair on the stage. "I'm going to make one just like it, except I'll desperately need to add more rhinestones."

Principal Love was standing at the microphone in the center of the stage. He was in the spirit of Pet Day, too, wearing a knitted scarf with purple alligators on it. Even the mole on his face had changed shape. Instead of looking like the Statue of Liberty, I swear it looked like a gerbil without a tail.

"Children, how exciting," he said. "Today PS 87 will finally have a new mascot, which will connect the animal kingdom with the kingdom of children, thus creating a space where children and animals coexist in what I like to call the kingdom of childimals."

"Did I just hear what I think I heard?" Frankie whispered to me.

"Yes, you did," said Ashley.

"We are now officially childimals," I whispered.

"What does that make Nick the Tick?" Frankie said. "He's already an animal."

"That's easy," I whispered back. "He's a jerkimal."

We cracked up, which was not such a good thing, because it caught the eye of Principal Love.

"Mr. Zipzer, would you mind taking your seat and not disrupting the proceedings," he said. "Unless you are a participant, you should be in the bleachers."

"I'm on my way, sir. I was just settling Team Cheerio down. Nerves are a little on edge today, as I'm sure you can understand. But here I am, on my way to my seat."

At the very instant, the doors to the multipurpose room flew open and Mason came bounding in like a Spalding pink high-bounce ball.

"Wait for me," he yelled. "I had to go to the bathroom and I couldn't get my underpants up."

Everybody burst out laughing. Mason stopped dead in his tracks with a surprised look on his face, wondering why everyone was laughing.

I put my arm around his shoulder, and whispered as quietly as I could, "Mason. When there's a group larger than two, we don't mention our underpants. And you haven't missed anything. Go take your place with Team Cheerio."

"Got it, Hank," Mason said, not even a little embarrassed. Then he darted off toward Ashley's outstretched hands and jumped right in her lap. What a great kid he is. He flashed me a thumbs-up and mouthed the words, "Cheerio's going to win!"

I didn't share his confidence. I mean, Cheerio

hadn't exactly been a star student in the training. And with so many kids crowding the room, I could see that he was feeling a little agitated. And when he's feeling agitated, it's police station, here we come again . . . if you know what I mean.

I climbed up into the bleachers and took a seat. The multipurpose room was almost full and all the kids actually seemed happy to be there and excited to see the contest. This was going to be a fun assembly, not like the one a couple weeks ago when a squeak-box opera singer from Brooklyn came and sang us a bunch of songs in German, wearing a blond wig and a helmet with horns.

I'm not kidding. The helmet had horns.

"Our first contestant is Luke Whitman," Principal Love said. "Luke, would you like to come forward and introduce your candidate for mascot?"

Luke went to the center of the stage area, squatted down on the floor, and placed a large green leaf in front of him. When he unwrapped the leaf, everyone leaned forward to see what he had.

"Eeuuwww," Rashid Nelson gasped. "It's one of those slimy things."

"I thought they were against the law," his buddy Connor called out.

A whole bunch of other boys from Mr. Sicilian's class cracked up and started to make gagging noises.

"It's called a slug," Luke said, glaring at them, "and it's like a snail with no shell. This one's name is Fritz."

"And what in particular is Fritz's talent?" Principal Love asked.

"He will leave a slime trail in the shape of a *p*, which as we all know is the first letter of PS 87."

"That is so incredibly weak," Nick McKelty yelled out from his place on the stage. I noticed that his Chihuahua, Fang, was shaking like a leaf in his lap.

"Oh yeah?" Luke fired back. "What can your dog in a rat suit do?"

Everyone in the multipurpose room started to laugh, which made McKelty steaming mad.

"Pupils," Ms. Adolf said, standing up from her chair on the judges' panel. "That's quite enough laughter to hold us for the rest of the afternoon. This mascot competition is not an occasion for fun. It is an educational experience through and through."

Boy, old Adolf knows how to stomp out a laugh before it even leaves your throat.

"And how long will this slime-trail-forming trick take?" Principal Love inquired.

"An hour and a half, if we're lucky," Luke said. "Depends if Fritz takes a pit stop, and we'll only know that if the color of the slime changes."

"I'm going to throw up," Katie Sperling said.

"I can feel it in the back of my throat now," her best friend, Kim Paulson, agreed. Those two do everything together.

"Why don't you take Fritz to the side of the room and allow him to continue, while we move on with the rest of the program," Principal Love suggested.

"Okay, but you don't know what you're missing," Luke shrugged.

"I'm quite sure we do," Principal Love said. "Now who's next?"

Frankie and Ashley both raised their hands at the same time.

"And who is your contestant?" Principal Love asked.

"Cheerio Zipzer," Frankie said.

"The hot-dog dog," Mason shouted out.

Everyone in the bleachers started to giggle, especially everyone in Mrs. McMurray's kindergarten class. I think they were happy that one of their classmates got a big laugh. All Ms. Adolf had to do was raise one finger on her grey hand, and that put an end to that. Every laugh in the room stopped mid-throat. I never thought silence could travel at the speed of sound.

Ashley led Cheerio up to the center of the stage area, and Frankie and Mason followed behind. Frankie was holding a baggy of bits of soylami, and Mason kept shaking his leg as if he was trying to get his tighty-whities to settle down.

I could see Cheerio's eyes scanning the audience, looking for me. Our eyes met, and my heart froze.

It was as if I could see into that crazy brain of his.

And what I saw was not good.

CHAPTER 25

But I was wrong.

Cheerio took the stage like a real champ. Ashley was holding his leash and he pranced out with his head held high and his tail waving back and forth as if he was saying, "Hello, everyone. Cheerio has arrived."

I know this sounds weird, because I'm not a dog and I don't really think like one. But I'm here to tell you that Cheerio knew this was his moment. He marched to the middle of the floor, sat his sweet little rump down, and waited for the command.

The kids in the audience sensed something great was about to happen, because they all leaned forward in their bleacher seats.

Ashley, Frankie, and Mason stood in a semi-circle around Cheerio and faced the kids.

"The dachshund was developed to smell,

chase, and flush out badgers," Ashley began in a clear, confident voice.

"From their burrows," Mason added in his very high kindergarten voice.

"Some historians believe dachshunds go all the way back to ancient civilizations," Ashley continued.

"Like Egypt," Mason added, very proud of contributing his fact.

Frankie flashed him a smile and gave him a thumbs-up. Ashley put her hand on his shoulder and gave him a light squeeze.

"The first real references to dachshunds came from books written in the 1700s," Frankie said, sounding like he knew all there was to know about wiener dogs.

"In Germany," Mason added.

Everyone in the audience chuckled. I could see Mrs. McMurray out of the corner of my eye, and she looked really impressed. Not only was Mason paying attention and focusing and doing a good job, but he had learned his facts perfectly. That's a lot for a five-year-old, especially one who has trouble in school and can't remember the alphabet. And I should know.

I also knew that I really wanted to be down there on the floor with them. On the one hand, I was so happy it was going well. But on the other hand, Cheerio was my dog and it was killing me not to be there with them.

"Before we begin our performance," Frankie said, "and on behalf of our entire team, we would like to thank Hank Zipzer, the founding member of Team Cheerio. Hank, please stand up and take a bow."

Every head in the multipurpose room turned and looked at me as I stood up. I took a big bow, probably deeper and longer than I should have, but can you blame me? It really felt good to have the old Zipzer attitude kick in.

"Sit down, Zipperdoofus," McKelty shouted from his chair. "Your stupid dog hasn't even done anything yet."

"That will be enough out of you, Mr. McKelty," Ms. Adolf said. "Please refrain from erupting like a volcano."

"Yeah, McKelty," I shouted back, before I could control my mouth. "Watch the lava dripping down your chin."

Everyone cracked up at that, but Ms. Adolf

was not having any of it.

"And that goes for you, too, Henry," Ms. Adolf said. "Might I remind all of you that we are not here to indulge in laughter."

At that very second, and I swear to you this is the truth, Randolf Bartholomew Irving Adolf let loose . . . and I'm afraid to say there is only one word to describe it and here goes . . . a *fart*. And not just a regular one, either. This one was a megaton.

It was so loud that Cheerio did a backflip from his sitting position, as if he was an Olympic gymnast. It didn't affect Luke Whitman's slug, however, that seemed to have stopped about halfway up his slimy *p*.

I don't know whether it was the odor or the trumpeting noise or both that upset McKelty's rat dog Fang, but whatever it was, that Chihuahua sprang off McKelty's lap and make a beeline for Cheerio, who had recovered from his backflip and was sitting there like a good dog, waiting to start his trick.

Before I had a chance to yell, "Watch out, killer Chihuahua on the loose," Fang sank his teeth into poor Cheerio's tail, and latched on like he was caught in a mousetrap. Cheerio was so startled, he started to spin in circles, chasing his tail at a rate faster than I've ever seen him do in his whole life. He built up speed with every revolution until he was just a whirring blur of motion.

"Stop, Cheerio," Mason yelled.

And can you believe it? Cheerio listened. He actually followed the command. He put on the brakes so fast that Fang was catapulted off his tail, like he had been shot from a slingshot. That little Chihuahua flew across the room and landed smack-dab on Nick McKelty's forehead, which knocked McKelty backward out of his chair. The two of them landed together in a heap on the floor.

Everyone was howling with laughter, and if there's one thing McKelty cannot stand it's to have people laughing at him. He jumped to his feet, held Fang above his head, and yelled out at the top of his lungs, "We meant to do that. That was our trick! Does my dog rock or what?"

"Right. If you meant to do that, then my name is Bernice," Frankie said.

The uncontrollable laughter that followed

made Fang shake with fear. And then it happened. He produced a yellow stream that came from . . . well, I think we all know where it came from . . . and ran down McKelty's arm into his shirtsleeve. It looked like he was getting a big sweat stain, but I don't have to tell you, that wasn't the truth.

Seeing that dog pee down McKelty's arm was maybe one of the greatest moments of my life. And if that wasn't sweet enough, it got even better when Principal Love ejected both of them—bully boy and rat dog—from the room.

"Mr. McKelty, I'm afraid you and your pet are disqualified for inappropriate and disruptive behavior unbefitting a mascot," he said. "Go to the office, call your mother, and *please* take a shower."

"Awww, why do I have to take a shower?" he said.

"Because, Mr. McKelty, you're starting to smell like the boys' room."

McKelty got up and lumbered out of the multipurpose room, but just before he left, he turned around and pointed to Cheerio.

"It's all your fault, wiener dog," he said.

But Cheerio didn't care. He just curled his lip and flashed him the old Zipzer family attitude.

That's my dog, I thought, *and I'm proud of him.*

CHAPTER 26

TRICKS PERFORMED BY THE NEXT FIVE CONTESTANTS IN THE COMPETITION

1. Ryan Shimozato brought in his parakeet named Larry, who stood on a ping-pong ball and rolled it almost the length of a ping-pong table, at which time Larry was so exhausted he fell off on his side and Ryan had to give him parakeet CPR. Just imagine Ryan blowing into Larry's beak. It was awesome to see.

2. Joelle Atkins dressed up her cat to look like a leopard in a leotard she painted. Joelle claimed that her cat could dial home on her cell phone. But instead, the cat pawed in the number for Miller's Dry Cleaners and caused Mr. Miller to burn a hole right through a white dress shirt he was pressing.

3. Salvatore Mendez brought in his snake and we watched it curl around his arm like an Egyptian bracelet. When Principal Love asked him what the trick was, he said, "Hey, my snake just turned into jewelry."

4. Chelsea Byrd brought in her algae-eater fish in a cloudy tank, and announced in her really shy voice that her fish, Suckerface, could eat all the algae and clear the water up. Principal Love told her that we didn't have time for that, since we were still waiting for Fritz the Slug to finish sliming his *p*.

5. The last trick was when Emily and Robert took Katherine out of her cage and . . . no, wait. What Katherine did doesn't deserve to be on a list. It should get a chapter of its own.

CHAPTER

27

Now, you know me.

I'm not a big fan of the reptile world, and most especially, not of one particular reptile that happens to live in the room next to mine. But you have to give credit where credit is due. And let me tell you, that hissing scaleball Katherine blew the roof off the multipurpose room.

The performance started with Emily giving a brief history of the iguana. Well, you know Emily. It wasn't brief, but it was thorough. She told way more about iguana life than everyone in the whole continent of North America would want to know. Then Robert, wearing his best clip-on tie (don't tell him, but it had some egg yolk dribbles on it from breakfast), opened Katherine's cage and placed her in the center of the stage. She opened her mouth and let out a hiss, which silenced the room quickly.

I had already seen the first part of her trick, where she balanced a grape on her snout with a Q-tip baton on top of the grape. But what I had never seen was her twirling the baton in her front claw while walking backward on her hind legs, as if she were a real drum majorette.

When she did that, the audience went wild. They erupted in applause and shouts, and I have to tell you, I was right there with them.

"Bravo, Katherine," I yelled.

I looked at Emily and Robert and they had identical smiles on their faces. They were so proud, they were grinning maniacs. And you know what? She's my sister, and I was proud, too.

Katherine was the last contestant, and it's a good thing. Who would want to follow that trick? No one, that's who.

We all waited quietly while the judges came up with their decision. Ms. Adolf and Mrs. McMurray huddled in the corner talking, while Randolf Bartholomew Irving Adolf kept trying to pull Ms. Adolf over to Cheerio. I think old Randolf wanted to be best friends with Cheerio, and I can't really blame him, because Cheerio is an extremely likeable little fellow. Likeable and tough, of course. I mean, he really took care of business when he taught that annoying Fang a thing or two. To tell you the truth, I didn't know he had it in him.

It didn't take them long to come up with their decision.

Ms. Adolf walked to the microphone with Mrs. McMurray beside her. She tapped the microphone to make sure the power was still on. It sounded like a clap of thunder.

"Pupils," she began. "Mrs. McMurray and I were most impressed with all the animal contestants except for the unfortunate tail-biting incident involving a certain disobedient Chihuahua. We now have our decision."

"Wait a minute," Luke Whitman called out from where he was kneeling next to Fritz. "My slug is so close to being finished."

"For our purposes, consider him finished," Ms. Adolf said. "We are out of time."

Poor Luke Whitman looked really disappointed, but he managed to cheer himself up by jamming his index finger up into his nose. That always works for Luke.

"Our first runner-up, and the pet who will be mascot should the winner be unable to fulfill its duties, is Ryan Shimozato's ping-pong-ball walking parakeet, Larry. Congratulations, Ryan and Larry."

The audience applauded, and everyone who could let out a bird whistle. Not to brag, but mine happens to be really great, so I let it fly, so to speak. All the while, I kept thinking, *Cheerio still has a chance.*

Ms. Adolf waited until the whistling was over, and then leaned into the microphone.

"The winner," she said with great drama, "and PS 87's new mascot for the next school year is . . ."

I looked at Frankie and Ashley and Mason. I could see that all three of them had their fingers crossed.

"Katherine . . . the wonderful, baton-twirling iguana entered by Emily Zipzer and Robert Upchurch."

Everyone burst into applause, and although I was disappointed for Cheerio, I had to applaud, too. I mean, Katherine *was* awesome.

While the audience went nuts, the strangest

thing happened onstage. Emily grabbed Robert, threw her arms around him, started jumping up and down, and planted a big kiss on his cheek. Right in front of everyone. Like we weren't looking.

"Emily Zipzer," Ms. Adolf said into the microphone. "Control yourself. There are no public displays of affection inside the walls of PS 87."

I looked over at Frankie and Ashley, and they just shrugged as if to say, "Hey, we did our best." But poor Mason looked really sad, which I could understand because having been a little kid myself, I know they don't like to lose. He slid off his chair onto the floor, put one arm around Cheerio, and scratched him behind his ear.

"You were so good at sitting," Mason said to him. "You're a good dog."

Mrs. McMurray tapped on the microphone and said, "Boys and girls, we do have one more important announcement."

Everyone quieted down to hear what it was.

"Under the circumstances," she said, "we felt that Cheerio Zipzer handled himself extremely

153

well. Even though Fang didn't keep his teeth to himself, Cheerio was respectful and restrained. He did not engage in a fight, and he showed consideration of another dog's feelings. As a result, we would like to confer on him the special award of Mr. Congeniality."

Mason shot up like a jack-in-the-box and started to yell, with his arms waving in the air.

"Cheerio is the best!" he chanted. "Cheerio is the best!"

Suddenly, he stopped yelling.

"What's Mr. Congeniality?" he said to Frankie.

"It means Cheerio is the friendliest, sweetest, nicest pet in the contest," Frankie said.

"Oh," Mason said. "Why didn't they just say that?"

Then he started jumping up and down again, yelling, "Cheerio is the best! Cheerio is the best!"

I couldn't resist. I ran out of the stands, charged up to Team Cheerio, and we all high-fived one another. We had to bend down a little so Mason could get in on the high-fiving.

And on his own, Cheerio walked right up

to Katherine and gave her a big, wet lick right across her snout.

The thing is, when you kiss an iguana, there are a lot of scales involved, and Cheerio did spend the next ten minutes spitting them out. But he didn't seem to mind. He just yipped and yapped and wagged his tail and licked everything that didn't lick him first.

He was one happy dog.

I guess that's the way it goes when you're Mr. Congeniality.

About the Authors

HENRY WINKLER is an actor, producer, director, coauthor, public speaker, husband, father, brother, uncle, and godfather. He lives in Los Angeles with his wife, Stacey. They have three children named Jed, Zoe, and Max, and three dogs named Monty, Charlotte, and Linus. He is so proud of the Hank Zipzer series that he could scream—which he does sometimes, in his backyard!

If you gave him two words to describe how he feels about the Hank Zipzer series, he would say: "I am thrilled that Lin Oliver is my partner and we write all these books together." Yes, you're right, that was sixteen words. But, hey! He's got learning challenges.

LIN OLIVER is a writer and producer of movies, books, and television series for children and families. She has created over one hundred episodes of television, four movies, and over twelve books. She lives in Los Angeles with her husband, Alan. They have three sons named Theo, Ollie, and Cole, and a very adorable but badly behaved puppy named Dexter.

If you gave her two words to describe this book, she would say "funny and compassionate." If you asked her what compassionate meant, she would say "full of kindness." She would not make you look it up in the dictionary.